There was a kind of bleak quiet while all hands stared at Idaho. The gunfighter's shrewd, part-closed eyes touched Sary, then moved unreadably at Grete. "You're the boss. Give your orders."

Grete didn't know if he was relieved or more worried, but this was no time to be unraveling riddles. "They know we're in front of them but maybe not how far. We're in no position to try any traps but we can, if we go at this right, throw those damn broncs right back in their laps. With this drive coming down on them, they're going to have to drag cotton and dig for the tules. They'll have no chance to pull up and make a fight of it—not if we hit them right. If we push these mares hard enough we ought to be onto them before they can get set."

Idaho, studying that, finally nodded. "They won't see our dust. But it's like to be hell with the clapper off when this drive smashes into them wild ones."

"We're going to have to chance that. We'll lose stock, but if we bring them up slow Bill's boys will empty some saddles. Shoot all you want, keep the mares bunched if you can, but once you're in the open don't stop," he said grimly, "or you won't ever leave there."

THE OVERLANDERS

Nelson Nye

LEISURE BOOKS 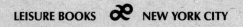 NEW YORK CITY

A LEISURE BOOK

Published by

Dorchester Publishing Co., Inc.
6 East 39th Street
New York, NY 10016

Printed in the United States of America

THE
OVERLANDERS

ONE

Scrape away their possessions, peel them down mother-naked, there'd be little to choose from between Grete Farraday and cattle king Crotton. Both were men who never backed down—who, knowing what they wanted, took the shortest route. But there was a difference. Crotton had what he wanted. He aimed to hang onto it.

He could ride all day and never get off his own range.

When you came right down to the brass tacks of the business it was this matter of range—of grass pure and simple—that had been back of the bust-up which had given the smaller roundabout spreads their first real chance to draw a full breath in years.

Grass, come right down to it, was all Crotton thought about—grass, and more Crotton cows to put onto it. That old sonofabitch wouldn't grant a prairie dog room for a burrow! It was what they all said.

Grete Farraday had finally got around to agreeing with them. But not until he'd had the facts of it pounded home to him. Up to then he'd more or less gone along with Crotton's notion grass was "fer them as can grab aholt and hang onto it." The shoe hadn't pinched till Grete got ready to pull it on.

For several years now he'd been ramrod for Crotton at a good round figure, most of which had gone into the bank. He wasn't getting no damn younger, country was filling up—even out on the no-account edges, and it had suddenly come over Grete, by God, it was time he was getting a wiggle on!

Plenty of owners had staked their top hands to one thing or another. He'd been a valuable man to Swallowfork, had had more than just something to do with it getting there. Experience had warned you couldn't count much on gratitude, but he had kind of figured they could make a deal of some sort. At the end of one long bitch of a day he'd gone up to see Crotton.

"I'm striking off on my own."

Crotton's hard eyes looked him over bright and narrowed. "In a couple of years. . ."

"I'm kind of set on doing it now."

Crotton dug out a pair of tumblers and a bottle. He set them up, stowing his away in one great apple-bobbin' gurgle. Grete sampled his and eyed the old bastard with a grudging respect. His gut felt like a bay steer had caught a hoof in it. Crotton growled, "All the best land's gone. Where the hell would you locate?"

"I got my eye on a piece."

"Some sodbuster's grant? Them boys'll make you hard to find."

Farraday refused to let the Old Man needle him. "I been thinking about cattle."

Crotton laughed.

Farraday got a little tight about the mouth. "I figure with a hundred head—"

"Shoestring!" Crotton snorted. "Damn country's overrun with greasy sackers now! Snot-nosed kids—women that look like they been drawed through a knothole! That what you're buckin' fer?"

8

Grete hadn't any too good a hold on his patience but he buckled his teeth around the words that reared up, chewed his cheek for a minute, then managed with an amazing mildness to say, "Vruthers set his top screw up with—"

"Vruthers! Jesus H. Christ!" Crotton jumped up, breaking wind like a mare clearing a three-rail fence. "Don't compare me to that old woman! I ain't about to start—"

"Nobody said you was," Farraday growled. "I was just—"

"An' if you think fer one minute. . ."

"For God's sake let me say what I was going to!"

"Don't snarl at me, you two-bit ingrate!" Veins stood out like ropes on Crotton's face. His chest heaved. The knuckles stuck out of his fists white as bone. "I shoulda seen all this," he said like Abraham discovering the viper. "I shoulda seen it comin' when I took you outa the hands of that Mex firin' squad—"

"By hell, you got your money's worth, mister!"

"It ain't his ass hangin' out of his pants makes a little man little. It's what he's got under his hair—like you, plain bone!" Crotton roared. "How far do you reckon you could get without me?"

It was the contempt in his voice, in those mean little eyes—the whole bullheaded arrogant look of him, that burned the last stayrope of Farraday's caution. He swung at the man, knocked him back and spread-eagled him against the wall with a crash that shook the whole house. The whites of Crotton's eyes rolled like a ringy bronc's. With a tremendous shout he leaped away from the wall, but Grete knew better than to let those bear-thick arms lay hold

9

on him. He dragged his gun. He shoved it into Crotton's belly. "Back off."

It seemed for a second as though the cowman would grab him anyway. The murderous flush fell away from his features and he let his arms come down, but he didn't step back and Farraday knew he never would.

"Get out!" Crotton growled, and it seemed to come clear from his boot tops. "Get out an' keep goin'. There's no room for you here—"

"We'll see," Farraday grinned. "You ain't the first damn hog I ever known. No matter how big you get there'll always be somebody that's a little bit bigger."

"You're done in this country," Crotton choked. "Ride out!"

Good advice, Farraday reckoned, thinking back on it now. But a man had his pride. He had started his spread right under their noses. Good land, real good—finest mountain-hemmed meadow in Crotton's Swallowfork iron. Every nickel Grete had went into it. They let him get the place built. How the old bastard must have laughed, he thought, cursing. They'd burned his shack, knocked his corrals into kindling— damned near got his hide on the fence. Probably would have, he figured, if Crotton had been along.

Perhaps the old pirate couldn't stomach the watching. More like he hadn't yet discovered Grete had filed on that lush meadow. He sure as hell was going to!

Or maybe Crotton did know. Maybe he figured this much of a lesson would be just as good as putting a slug through him, that Grete would be so almighty thankful to get out with his health he wouldn't stop this side of Panama.

In a way he didn't blame Crotton too much —it was that kind of country. All the old bastard had was a sixshooter title. Fear of Crotton's gunnies was all that was keeping Swallowfork intact. If the threat of Crotton's wrath were set aside one time, every sucker he'd put the spurs to or scared away would come a-runnin'.

But Crotton shouldn't have made a fool of him—Grete could imagine the grins going round as men discussed his short tenure as an owner. It was plain he couldn't buck Crotton without he had help. He'd get no help in Arizona. Not even Curly Bill—and he could mass a hundred riders—wanted any piece of a Swallowfork hoedown. Bill's style was hit and run. He wasn't about to try anything that would put King Crotton after him.

Grete didn't want Bill's kind of help anyway. Too unreliable, too hard to get shut of. He had in mind tying up with some really big auger, some brand that was just as skookum as Swallowfork but would leave him the part of Crotton's range he had filed on.

What Grete really wanted was enough hard cash for guns and wire—apt to come high back in Arizona in the shadow of Swallowfork. He'd been hoping to get hold of some here in New Mexico but would go, by God, clean to Texas if he had to.

He'd got around to thinking in terms of Murphy-Dolan, a pair of sharp customers kicking up dust along the Pecos. According to all tell they'd just about got the store business cornered and was branching out now into horses and cattle. For a toehold on Swallowfork they might be nudged into giving him a hand.

This, leastways, was what he'd been counting on; but Lincoln County was clear the

11

other side of nowhere. Another night was closing in, the fifth he'd put behind him; and any time at all it might come into Crotton's head to put a man of his own into Farraday's meadow and pre-empt that quarter section around the springs Grete's claim was filed on. They could pass it around he had pulled his freight, and no white-collared clerk was going to stand off a man like Crotton.

Farraday cursed. He could talk about going clean to Texas but he didn't have anything like that much time. It could damned well be too late already! If he only kept on to Murphy-Dolan's he was going to have to cross the Jornada, that dreaded Journey to Death desert most way-farers skirted as they would the plague. Take another full day and maybe half a night and—without he'd been lied to—not a drop of water on it.

He shook his canteen which, by the slosh, was half-empty. He knew he had scarce enough grub for one feed; but it was the dun had him worried. He scowled at the billowing golden haze which he knew was blown sand touched up by the last dying shafts of the sun. Wind out there could blow your goddamn pants off. A fool's gamble, he reckoned; but he had come too far to be turned aside now.

He kicked the gelding ahead and then pulled up, staring.

The sun was suddenly gone. Coming out of the swirling dust like gray ghosts were the heads-down, shambling shapes of spent horses, two or three practically staggering.

Hearing no sound, Farraday rubbed his eyes to see if he was dreaming; but still they came, plodding out of that murk, grotesquely, incredibly—not mustangs but hot-bloods! He cursed in astonishment as more and still more of them come out of the dust.

Now a stallion flung up his head in hoarse challenge, a shift in the wind fetching the sound to Grete faintly. The gelding, crouched between Grete's knees, trembled. The hot-bloods stopped, wheeling uncertainly, their manes streaming out like ragged banners in the gloom. A wagon appeared with high sides and tarp roof, riders abruptly materializing back of it.

Grete counted four and caught the glint of shifted rifles; saw two of the riders spur out to cut around the stock and hold it—a needless precaution to Grete's way of thinking. The remaining pair sat motionless, considering him with a rock-hard attention as, with lifted hand, he put the dun toward them.

"What outfit's this?" he asked, coming up.

No one spoke for a couple of minutes. Then the elder of the pair, a man gaunt enough to have climbed through the gut of a needle, swiveled an amber-flecked stare and made an irritable shift of his weight in the saddle. "You got a plaster on this chunk of hell?"

Farraday, grinning, folded his hands on the horn in token of his peacefulness and shook his head. "Nope. Just seeing the country, as the feller said. You have any trouble making the crossing at the Pecos?"

The gaunt man looked as though it hadn't got through to him. The other one said with a willful arrogance: "Burn him down, Idaho!"

It whipped Farraday's tightening look around. Before he could wheel or put his resentment in words the voice of a woman came out of the wagon. "What is it, Ben? What does he want?"

The bull-chested one said, "Another damn rustler—"

Farraday's knees drove the dun hard against him; but as Grete reached for the fellow, the gaunt one said, "You tired of livin', mister?"

Looking down the bore of that Henry repeater Farraday reluctantly backed the dun off. It was the chunky man did the crowding now. Beefy jowls gone dark with blocked spleen, he was rearing back in the safety of that rifle to fistmark Grete when the voice from the wagon said under his elbow, "I'll handle this, Ben."

His nibs didn't like it but the girl didn't seem to care about this. In her middle twenties, there was something indefinable about her which, by Farraday's lights, did not fit a proper lady. It had nothing to do with her appearance which was lanky, crisp, redheaded. She had a pinto vest clapped round her and a .44 riding the swell of one hip.

She sized Grete up with a tightening look and the red mouth below the smoky hue of that glance turned hard as a well-chain. "What do *you* want?"

"Pardon me all to hell," Grete scowled. "Must be Sidewinder Day where you come from!"

The chunky Ben, leaning down with a snarl, was fixing to put in his oar when she said: "Be still." Bold eyes raked Grete's face with a livening interest. "What *are* you here for?"

"Counted on getting me some dope about the Pecos."

She said, too quick, "We didn't come by the Pecos," and their eyes gripped and locked, Farraday's openly calling her a liar, mocking her, diving bright with malice to the pasterns of Ben's horse. She looked at the crusted mud on

14

its fetlocks and the red mouth curved in a slow wide smile. She stepped back a piece, watching him. "We'll eat here, Idaho. Have Barney get a fire started." When the man went off she said, "I'll talk with you."

The chunky Ben had hell in his gullet. Cheeks thinned with anger, he said, fingering the butt of his pistol, "No, by God! We'll have no truck with rustlers!"

The girl's head came around. "Are you running this now?"

"Time I did, by the looks. As your closest relation—"

"I wouldn't presume on that, Ben." Still-faced, she looked up at him. "When I want your advice I'll ask for it." She said to Grete, "We'll talk in the wagon."

He swung down, letting go of the reins. Ignoring the man's affronted scowl he moved along in her wake, trying to work some of the saddle cramp out of his legs while openly admiring the natural swing of her hips. He climbed after her into the bed of the wagon, feeling the lurch of it, catching the shine of her hair in the match's flare, watching her poking its flame in a lantern. There was a bunk, a stove for heat, and a bank of built-in cupboards. She pushed a hand toward the bunk. "Sit down. I'm Sary Hollis." Her eyes came around and up at him coolly. "Flying H."

"Grete Farraday," he said, not trying the bunk, not bothering either to take off his hat.

She wasn't his idea of pretty. Her jaw was too square, the red mouth too determined. She looked tired, he thought, as he looked her over. Probably was. But the queer something he had sensed from the start of this business was still riding her, crackling through her tone like

15

broken branches.

"Would it help if I undressed?"

He felt the heat in his cheeks. "Reckon," he said, "I asked for that," and, ducking his head, put out a foot for the step.

"You said you were traveling. . ."

He twisted to look at her.

"Are you free to take a job or are you one of those pilgrims who can't work for a woman?"

"I've got about all the job I can handle."

He turned again to leave and once more her words laid hold of him. "I could make it worth your while."

He listened, the rich timbre of her voice wandering through the closed doors of his mind. This wasn't what he wanted, but she had a crew and she had stock. Eyes half-shut, Grete Farraday considered. Four men, if they were handled right. . . He thought of Ben and that gaunt one, Idaho; but he was still a far piece from Lincoln and he might get turned down there. "Let's hear your proposition."

She hid the lifting surge of her spirit. "Good horses in Texas are a drug on the market. But in Arizona, I've been led to believe, a really top horse will just about fetch anything you might ask for. I'd like to get these Shilohs over there."

He shook his head. "You've been misinformed."

"About what?"

"Offhand I'd say a lot of things. You'd be lucky to get through with this stock. The country's lousy with owlhooters."

She smiled at his gun, brought her glance up and said, "You can have four mares, your own pick, if we make it."

Grete didn't know whether to laugh or be insulted. "Not many settlers can afford to pay anything like what you'd ask. Your market's with the sporting crowd and unless your outfit's fast on the trigger—"

"All right. I've got eighty bred mares—the stud is by Steel Dust out of a daughter of Old Billy. You can have one-tenth of all the mares we arrive with and half the foals that are dropped on the way."

Sureness seemed to be a part of this woman and he sensed something here, something carefully hidden, that she knew and he did not. He studied her carefully. "I wouldn't of took you for a drinking woman."

Sary Hollis laughed. "It's a deal?"

"No."

Her look winnowed down. He felt the weird creep of an unfamiliar excitement. There was something about this full-bodied woman. . . "The only deal I'd make with you would be an even-Steven share, fifty-fifty, straight across the board." He saw the shock in her face, the rebellious fury. "And there'd be only one mouth passing orders—mine."

He saw the knuckles go white against her fists. "Go ahead," he said, and grinned derisively. In the clutch of silence she stared back at him, hating him. With chin tilting bitterly she pulled back her shoulders. "That's your price?"

"That's it."

She considered the uncompromising cut of his jaw, the beard-stubbled cheeks, the solid length of his body, yellow-haired, bold as brass, with a splatter of dust streaked across granite features.

She drew a shuddering breath and bent her head to hide its secrets.

He could feel her revulsion, the cold blaze of

17

her hate. These were nothing. There was only one thing he cared about—getting that meadow land away from Crotton. If her crew and horses could be bent to that purpose. . .

TWO

His eyes kept watching her face with grim patience until, abruptly fed up with it, he pushed open the door and felt again for the step.

"When do you propose to take over?"

He left the foot where it was. "Soon as your boys get some chuck under their belts."

"You drive a hard bargain. I doubt if your knowledge of the country and conditions can be worth so steep a price."

But she was hooked and both of them knew it. Grete said, to allow her some vanity, "You figure on getting more than that." He wondered how far he could trust her and what the situation was between her and that Ben. It stood to reason she was covering up something.

His glance caught sight of a pendant cameo swung from a fine gold chain about her neck. The backing—some sort of red agate or petrified wood—appeared thick enough to be hollow inside—not that he gave a damn whose picture she carried.

She kind of jumped when he snorted. He growled, "What are you scairt of?" and saw her visibly stiffen, watched her eyes back off and try to hide behind scorn.

She pushed out a hand. "I'll keep my part of—"

"And I'll get you there."

She turned away, hating him, hating herself even more but no less determined than when, quitting Lubbock, she'd left everything behind.

She could imagine his eyes prying through the piled-up silence. *Why doesn't he leave?* her mind cried edgily. "After we've eaten," she said, "I'll tell them."

"Probably take a little time to get this stock sold. You got a place in mind to work from?"

She hated to admit it. "I hadn't thought of that."

"I've got plenty of grass."

It wasn't until the words tramped through her mind a second time that she caught hold of their significance. It brought her head up sharply. "You've got a ranch?" She stood completely still. "Half of it's mine then—that's what you said! Straight across the board, an even fifty-fifty."

The glint of his half-shut eyes seemed to mock her but he admitted her claim with a careless nod. "That's right." He grinned. "Be like traveling in double harness. . . Well, I'll be around."

He ducked through the door, leaving a squeak of dry hinges.

She couldn't think why she should feel so disquieted. She'd looked for losses, and three years with Tate. . . Even with the horse money halved she would be in better shape than she could ever remember. She'd have half that ranch!

She tried to hug the thought to her but the glow the prospect warranted someway wouldn't quite come alive. And it wasn't the succession of faded hopes, or the lost dreams remembered, or the years tied down to a sick man and debts. . . Was a woman ever able to pick up the pieces?

She sat down on the bunk, staring unseeingly at the wall. It wasn't even the thought of the law catching up—she'd got used to that phantom hovering over her now. Like her worries about Ben and the misgivings aroused by the men he had chosen. She got up, still dissatisfied, to look in the piece of cracked mirror, searching the eyes that stared back. *He'll do it*, she thought. *He'll get them through if anyone can*.

Grete Farraday. She tried the name on her tongue, unaccountably shivering. He knew she was running. His kind would see that no outfit would take horses through the Jornada without they were fools or trying to lose something back of them.

Her glance touched the baling wire holding together one leg of the bunk. She had always been strong but would she be strong enough?

What are you scairt of?

Yes. That was it. He had the alarmingest eyes she had ever looked into.

When Farraday left he stood a moment on the step to bring the campsite into focus. He saw the yellow wink of firelight and, against the shifting dark of stock, the shape of a man crouched over a skillet.

His glance sought the roundabout shadows. Rope-hardened fingers joggled his pistol, resettling it more to his liking while he stood with cocked head listening into the dark, corraling and correlating each scratch of sound that came out of the night's deep stillness.

This concern with little things was the price a man paid for having been top screw at

Swallowfork, for having been the one who implemented Crotton's orders. The twist of an eye, a shifting shadow—even the way a man belched in this country could have astonishing significance and spell that thin shred of difference between continued breathing and the final end of hope.

This was what experience had taught.

Now Farraday, sighting his horse, moved toward it, recollections of Sary Hollis uneasily tugging his attention from the maze of details he must scrap or someway alter to fetch the focus of new facts into line with his original problem.

The girl had fled some kind of trouble which might not or might come down on him. This crew had to be evaluated, tightened, each man of it seen in his proper perspective. There was no screen for half-tones in Farraday's head when it came to separating sheep from goats. There'd be the natural animosities of change. The girl's character would have to be reckoned with. This bunch wouldn't willingly be reconciled to him.

He was half minded for a moment to shove on for Lincoln, pride and time being the biggest things that stood in his way. There was also the possibility Murphy-Dolan wouldn't go for it. He expected he'd be wiser to make the best of what he had. Speaking to the dun he caught up the reins and, with them contained in his grip on the horn, bent to twist the stirrup for the toe of his boot.

The dark wheel of a shape came suddenly beside him. The hard end of something slammed into his ribs and gaunt Idaho's voice, honed thin by the rasp of repression, fell like cold fingers across the arch of Grete's spine. "One grunt an' you get it!"

22

A leaping anger pushed its brash urge at Farraday, but a man didn't argue with a gun-snout reminding him how close he stood to death.

"What're you tryin' to pull around here? Talk, you damned maverick!" The gun dug in harder. "I got ears in my head!"

"Then you know what the deal is."

"She's not for the likes of you!" In the dancing gleam of the leaping flames the man's raw-red cheeks showed the twist of fury. "You ever touch her—"

A shadow crossed his firelit face. He quit talking. The gun left Grete's ribs as Ben's chunky shape stepped out of the dark. "What's up?" Ben cried, at once sharply suspicious.

Idaho, squeezing his thin lips together with a final black look, stamped off without answering. Ben, half-turned to peer after him, swung back. "All right," he snarled. "We got enough of your kind around here. Hit the saddle."

"Maybe," Grete said, "you better talk with her, too."

"Don't give me your sass!" The man took a threatening step but pulled up when he caught the bared shine of Grete's teeth. "What's that supposed to mean?"

"From here on in I'm bossing this drive. That clear enough for you?"

The man fell back as though Farraday had struck him. His mouth sprang open as for a mighty yell but nothing came out and Grete, recalling what he'd seen of this fellow, found no cause for revising his estimate. Behind Ben's brawn, behind the arrogance and bluster, was a soul that packed a fiddle string where a man's guts ought to be. Grete half-cocked a fist and

23

had all the proof he needed when the man, white-checked and shaking, stumbled back with an animal whimper.

Although it made him crawl with disgust and revulsion, Farraday watched until Ben got into blackness too deep to keep track of him. Grete climbed into leather then and, moving back into heavier shadows, cut around to the far side of the fire.

This outfit had a second wagon, visible from here. A kind of combination chuck and supplies wagon, from the back end of which the man by the fire had unpacked Dutch ovens in addition to the skillet and was now busily engaged throwing together a meal. He had a patch over one eye and, although Grete wasn't able to make out his features, this and a kind of swoop and jerk to the way he moved brought to mind a picture of Stevenson's Long John Silver.

A man rode in from the dark bulk of horses and flung out of the saddle with a weary man's grumbling, dropping down by the fire. Grete's eyes sought and found the window light from Sary's wagon, saw its gleam blocked out and Ben's shape briefly limned in the glow from the opened door. Movement pulled Grete's head around. He watched gaunt Idaho come up and squat down. The cook limped over; and now, with all four of them placed, Grete's eyes narrowed.

Who the hell was watching those horses!

The girl evidently had more men than he had seen. Even with that stallion it stood to reason they would have at least one man keeping an eye out. That suggested five men in this outfit. Perhaps more.

He kept turning this over in his mind, not liking it. Three competent men could have moved this stock handily. Actually the stud

24

would be doing all the work. Why had the girl brought so large a crew? Out of fear of thieves or because of what had driven them to cross the Jornada?

For the first time Grete wondered if he had bitten off more than he could chew with this outfit.

The girl's door fanned light and she stepped out, the big Ben trailing her. Grete moved the dun up to the fire and swung down, loosening the cinch a notch and slipping off the bridle so the horse could more comfortably browse. The crew made a business of elaborately ignoring him.

The girl came up with Ben. She said, "You better watch that dun. If he gets near those mares. . ."

"He won't."

She looked dubious, but shrugged. The fellow beside Idaho had got to his feet when she appeared but the gaunt man stolidly continued to hunker on his bootheels, sifting buff dirt through his gunfighter's fingers. "This—" Sary said, waving a hand at him, "is Idaho. Cook answers to 'Patch'; the dark-faced one is Frijoles. Boys, meet Grete Farraday."

The cook, grunting, bent over his ovens. Frijoles managed a frozen-faced nod but Idaho kept right on sifting dirt, his amber-flecked stare never lifting above it. "I'm overcome, too," Grete said, holding his temper. His thumb jerked at Ben. "What about this fellow—he too important for a common man to know?"

He was ashamed of this churlishness as soon as he'd got the words out; but the girl, chin high, said, "I'm sorry—Ben Hollis," almost as if it choked her. The name caught at Grete's notice and he stared, glance narrowing, from one to the other. "Your brother?"

25

"Brother-in-law." The chunky man's toothy grin was smugly compounded of mockery and triumph. "Her husband's brother," he proclaimed pontifically, "and as such. . ."

But Farraday swept the man out of his mind. He was glaring at the girl, feeling cheated and put upon. By withholding the fact of her marriage . . . He said, grinding down on his anger, "And where would your husband be now, ma'am? If he's out with those horses—"

"Tate's dead," the man's brother said, leering maliciously. "And so, as head of the family—"

"You own these horses?"

"Not exactly," the man bridled, "but—"

"You paying this crew?"

Hollis said irritably, "I've got—"

"Mister," Grete said, "you haven't got nothing but an oversized mouth."

Hollis' face blanched. "You can't—"

"I've heard enough out of you," Farraday growled, and put his look roughly across the rest of them, darkening the cheeks of the chin-strapped Frijoles, forcing the cook's single eye to swerve aside. Gaunt Idaho got up holding his raw look expressionless and Farraday said, throwing his words at the girl, "It's about time we got some things out in the open. You better tell them about that proposition you made me."

"Yes!" Sary said too quickly, almost frantic. "Mr. Farraday knows Arizona. He understands conditions, the people . . . He's got a ranch in that country—half of it will be mine and I'm giving him half the horses . . . the mares, that is, and half their increase." She met the hard looks defiantly. "That's the deal. He's boss of this now. You'll take your orders from him."

Silence shut down, a stillness turned ugly

with unspoken resentments. Farraday, turning over what the years had taught him, felt the quiet become brittle, stretched insufferably thin. Only his eyes, hard as gun muzzles, held them; and then Idaho, shoving Frijoles out of his path, came in front of him, glowering, with a rattle of rowels. "You got that in writin'?" he said over his shoulder.

Sary sighed. "His word is good."

"Sure of that, are you?" A sneer curled Idaho's lips. "It looks like to me you don't know who your friends are." With his breath reaching deeper he settled forward a little, the bright burn of his stare grinding into Grete's temper like the clamp of a wheel-lock. "If this jasper's Farraday, he's been trailin' with the biggest pack of thieves in Arizony!"

Swallowfork he meant, Grete guessed, and saw a great leap of joy drive through the chunky Ben; but Sary took the play away. "Then," she said coolly, "he won't mind rubbing elbows with our Texas breed of coyotes. Dish up, Patch, we've got a long night ahead of us."

"That's right," Grete nodded. "We'll be pushing on soon as you fellows get out of the nose bags."

He turned away from the man, suspecting even as he did so that courage and quick-thinking weren't going to be enough. And he was right. Ben's gaunt gunfighter had got the stage set and wasn't minded, with Frijoles and the cook looking on, to be left like a snot-nosed kid with his pants down.

As Farraday wheeled to step over to the fire, Idaho's right hand slammed for his hip while his left, snaking out, latched onto Grete's shoulder, spinning him around. In Idaho's plan this was intended to set Grete up to where, startled and off-balance, he'd make a pass for his gun and catch a slug for his trouble. Grete was way ahead of him.

What actually happened was too fast for eyes to follow. When the gunfighter's grip seized hold of his shoulder, Grete, shifting balance for the yank he knew would come, anchored the entire hundred and eighty pounds of his weight to one braced boot. Using this for a fulcrum he came around with the force of a catapult.

A flying fist crashed into Idaho's jaw. The pistol sailed out of his jerked-wide hand. Shocked surprise and momentum carried him into the fire where panic crossed his legs and pitched him yelling down into the dust.

The next thing he knew he was being jerked upright. Something exploded in his face like a Fourth of July rocket. He plunged down a well of shrieking blackness filled with a blur of pin-wheeling lights.

When he came to again Farraday stood over him with a dripping bucket. "I've seen drowned rats that looked prettier," Grete said, "but I doubt if I ever come onto a wetter one. You still need convincing who's the boss around here?"

When Idaho didn't speak up fast enough to suit him Grete swung the oaken bucket, breaking it against the side of the man's head. A great shout broke out of him. He got both arms hugged about his bloody face and, rolling out of Grete's reach, staggered onto his feet.

Grete straightaway went after him, driving a fist hard against that stretched belly, fetching a knee up into Idaho's face. It was a broken-nosed smear but Farraday hammered it three more times without mercy, knowing if he went light on this man he would have the whole pack of them soon to contend with. The gunfighter's head rocked with each punishing impact. He hooked his spurs and fell heavily, moaning.

Grete, rubbing cut knuckles, prowled around till he found Idaho's pistol. He stepped over and thrust it at the gray-cheeked Ben. "When he acts like he's got some sense give it back to him."

He wheeled away. "Let's eat."

THREE

Nobody looked to have much hunger.

The gunfighter after a while got up and went dragging off into the dark; Farraday, knowing the risk, permitted this, not even bothering to move away from the fire. Having no idea what kind of food he was putting into him, he went on with his eating, forcing the stuff down, disregarding the girl and the men's covert glances. As he had reminded himself earlier, there was just one thing he wanted out of this—the means of forcing Crotton to come to terms or, failing that, smashing him.

When Frijoles got up to toss his tin in the wreck pan Farraday said, "How many we got out there watching that stock?"

Frijoles was a wiry shape beneath a chin-strapped sombrero. His dark, whiskered face shied away. *"Dos hombres, senor."*

"Find Idaho and send them in." Grete wheeled. "My horse is ready to be watered, Ben."

The Mexican rode off. Ben Hollis glared. Hatred poured out of his eyes strong as tears. A violent agony of choice broke out across his beefy cheeks but in the end he got to his feet. When he came back, Farraday said, "Catch up your horse and get out there with them."

Cook said from the tailgate, "How far we goin'?"

"Another six or eight miles."

"You figurin' to make Stein's Pass tomorrow night?"

"I don't figure to make that place at all."

Patch wiped his hands on the piece of smeared canvas he was using for an apron, reached around to get hold of the strings. "That bein' the case you can pay me off now."

"No one's quitting this drive without he's flat on his back."

The cook's single eye flared up like blown lampflame. "You sound like that brass-checks bunch in Californy! Man's got some rights, by Christ!"

Farraday's teeth gleamed behind tight lips.

A fellow rode in from the direction of the stock, picking Grete out with a wide-eyed stare. "Barney Olds," he said, dropping out of the saddle. He was tousle-haired and growthy in a gangling, awkward and unsure sort of way; big for his age, which wasn't over fifteen. Wood packer, probably, back where they'd come from.

Farraday looked at Ben. "Anything wrong with your hearing?"

Hollis' eyes slid away. The angry memory of something blackly laced with shame wrote itself across his cheeks but Grete's hard stare was too much for him. He wheeled around and stamped over to the kid's pony, slammed aboard and rode off.

The kid, studying Farraday, filled a tin at the tailgate, got himself a scald of java and hunkered down beside the fire. Grete felt the girl's regard, but kept his glance on the cook, now viciously scraping at his ovens with a fire

31

hook. Grete said to the kid, "Thought there was two of you out with those horses."

"Rip's got his eats with him."

It occurred to Grete he would be a heap smarter to get this deal down on paper but he was leery of mentioning this lest the girl, perhaps already regretting it, make of the suggestion an excuse to back out. He watched her get up and drop her things in the wreck pan. He looked away when she wheeled, ignoring her approach.

"Could I bother you a moment?"

He said ungraciously, "What is it?"

"Come over to the wagon."

She took his arm when they got into the dark. This bothered him too. He resented the ease with which she made him aware of her. She felt his antagonism and stopped, stepping back from him. She fetched a crackle of paper from a pocket of her riding skirt. "We might as well do this right while we're at it."

The paper was folded around the stub of a pencil. He took it into the light, the twist of a smile tugging his lips as he read. It was his side of the bargain, making over half the ranch in exchange for half the stock and the rights vested in him as trail boss. He masked his elation, appearing to hesitate. Coming back, he said, "And the part I'm to keep?" She held it out and they swapped. "Was it a steal you ran from," he said, "or a killing?"

Her chin came up. "I don't recall asking you."

He felt it go into him, gaff, shaft, and haul rope. Whatever else she might be this girl was no fool. He glared, halfway hating her. "What's that kid doing here?"

"Weren't you ever his age?"

He had no patience with sentiment. "I must

have been loco to tie myself up with this kind of outfit!" He looked at her bitterly, catching dead-on the frozen stare she sent back to him.

"I don't care what you think—what you've been, even. But there is one thing I won't tolerate from you and that's treachery!"

It brought him up short.

He thought in that moment to catch a flutter of hoofs, but with the wind pirootin' round and her paying no attention he supposed he must have imagined it. He said, "What the hell are you talking about?"

"Stein's Pass."

"What about it?"

"I heard what you said." Her eyes were on him narrowly. "How else do you propose to get through those mountains?"

He reckoned again to be hearing that faint plop of hoof sound and twisted his head without adding to his knowledge. He swung back to her. "You hear anything?"

"Let's stay with the steer we've got hold of."

The sound came to Farraday plainly then, nearer now, almost up to the camp, but the freight of anger and suspicion in her tone dragged his caution away from it. "There's a trail," he said, "through from Animas—"

"Forty miles out of our way," she said flatly.

"For an outsider, by God, you've got some mighty queer savvy."

Her chin tipped up. "Wait over there," she called, lifting her voice. "I'll be through here directly." Her eyes came back to Grete. "What is there at Stein's you're so scared to face up to?"

Farraday reddened. "Not scared," he said. "It just don't make sense—"

"Then I'll see if we can't find some!" She brushed past him sort of panting and went, half-running, toward the fire.

Farraday, tramping after her, was riled enough to taste it when the shape of the horse drawn up by the wagon turned out to be Idaho. Grete heard her say to the man as he stepped into the firelight, "Is there any good reason for avoiding Stein's Pass?"

The gunfighter, hunching thin shoulders, gave Farraday a battered grin. "Ain't never heard of none," he said through puffy lips. "But then I ain't never rode for Swallerfork, neither."

Sary's glance, bitterly furious, lashed from one to the other. "I didn't ask for riddles!"

"Why, ma'am, there's no riddle here. Mister Farraday's got his own nest to feather." The narrow amber-flecked stare swept over Grete with a wicked maliciousness. "You can't buy his kind. He'll use you as long as it suits his ends, then find some prettier, younger woman—"

Grete went for the man in one slashing leap. The horse threw its head up, sidling, snorting, the flames flinging out a skittering light from the barrel of the pistol nakedly focused on Grete's chest.

Idaho's eyes jeered openly now. Underneath his thumb the hammer came up. "Put those hands on me, bucko, whenever you're a mind to."

The threat of the gun held Farraday rooted but the strain showed through the thin slant of his cheeks. Incredibly then he laughed at the man, a shocking sound in that brittle quiet. "Believe me," he said, eyes granite hard, "if there was any real point to it that gun wouldn't stop me."

Strangely Idaho appeared to accept this.

He had the advantage, of course, of looking

34

into Grete's face, a thing the girl could not do, being off to one side. Her glance swept them both with a cold disdain. "We'll go by Stein's."

They'll go," Grete said, "the way I tell them to go." He turned his back on her wrath. "Get those horses strung out." He waved the gunfighter away. "You there, kid, hitch up—"

"Barney, stay where you are," Sary Hollis cried furiously. "If we've got business at Stein's we're going there! Irv, did you locate those buyers?"

Trailing her stare Farraday saw the man then. Back where broad shadows helped cloak his motionless presence he stood with gripped reins against a roan horse like something straight out of Scripture. There was that patriarchal look to his still face, that peculiar blend of vision and authority, of assurance in adversity which comes of righteous suffering.

His name was Irv French. Grete, on Crotton's orders, had chased the sonofabitch out of the country for running his brands on other men's cattle.

FOUR

"Yes," French said, "I've lined up four."

A sigh came out of Grete too deep for words.

He had played in hard luck from the start of this deal and now to be saddled with a joker like French seemed almost more than a man could take. "Slick" was the name folks had found for Irv French and that he was still above ground attested to its accuracy. He could twist truth around to where you'd pick black for white, and not only pick it but pass it on for gospel. He could do things . . . Hell! It was plain enough now where the girl had got her slant. He was slicker than slobbers—give the devil his due. Not even King Crotton had been able to catch him out.

Farraday said to the girl, "This one of your outfit?"

"Mr. French kindly offered—"

"I'll be he did!" Grete's mouth was tight. "He's the helpingest gent you will ever run into. By God, you sure pick 'em!"

A resentful defiance burned into her look and anger boiled up through her cheeks like a fever. Aroused she was handsome in a wild sort of way that got its teeth in old hungers. Grete said irascibly: "You got any idea what you've let this drive in for?"

"I don't care for your tone. If you're implying Mr. French is a crook, I don't believe it."

"There you are, Irv—a real testimonial. Given by a woman of unimpeachable antecedents." Farraday's look held a biting contempt.

Sary's eyes turned black. French brought his fullpaunched shape out of the shadows, the roan horse ambling along at his heels like a dog. There was a half-smiling negligence about this old man's movements, a contained tolerance of expression, that made Grete's words sound cheap and childish. "Getting kicked off Swallowfork must have soured your outlook, Farraday."

Farraday's bitter eyes found the girl. "So it was Irv put the notion of Stein's into your bonnet. You got any more cute surprises tucked away up your sleeve?"

"No sense taking your spleen out on her."

That was French. Grete ignored him. "You believe that bull about four buyers?"

Her chin came up. "It will be easy enough to prove."

"Sure. Be easy, all right. Easy as dropping out of sight in a bog hole."

"No point scaring her with Bill," French said. "Even if he was there I'd have no trouble doing business—"

"Save your breath. You won't be doing any with him this trip. That stock isn't going anywhere near Stein's."

The chunky Ben drifted up and put a shoulder against the wagon.

Sary cracked her knuckles. "May I say something?"

Grete, swallowing the bile that rose up in him, said, "Go ahead." He caught the fire-honed glint of Idaho's eyes and got ready for trouble.

The girl said, "This Bill, apparently, is some sort of outlaw?"

"You're learning fast."

"Well . . . But if Mr. French can do business with him—"

"Anyone can do business with him. If they don't mind being paid off with bullets."

The glint of the gunfighter's eyes, shifting, sharpened. But French, smiling, shrugged and said lightly, "Bill ain't much different than anyone else—"

"He don't have two heads, if that's what you mean."

French didn't let Grete's sarcasm throw him. He grinned at the girl. "Your friend Farraday don't like him, being politically tethered where the grass, come spring, doesn't get above his ankles—Lord, I don't blame him. If I was in his fix I wouldn't care for Bill either."

"He's talking about *Curly* Bill," Grete said grimly, and saw Idaho stiffen. Sary looked confused. Ben pulled his shoulder away from the wagon, walked around back of Idaho, and stopped. "What kind of fix is that?" he said.

"Well . . ." French sighed. He pushed out his lips and looked around as though embarrassed. "I didn't suppose it was any secret he's been lifting other folks' cattle." His glance found the girl's. "He was ramrod at Swallowfork till Crotton got onto him—no telling how much he got away with while he had the crew out scouring the country, trying to cover up by making out it was me. Someway Bill got his signals crossed—he was getting rid of the stuff, splitting with Grete here whatever it fetched. A message from Bill was delivered to Crotton. Your friend," French grinned, "barely got out."

It never occurred to Farraday a denial to anything so preposterous was called for until he saw Sary's eyes. That same drawn-away kind of look was on the rest of them. He was branded, and nothing he might say after this would change their minds.

The girl's eyes went through him like the steel points of daggers. "You said something about grass..." She was looking at French. "Am I to understand his ranch—"

It was the brightening lift of French's rolled-back stare that pulled Grete into an awareness of danger. This wasn't the worst the man could do. The lack of Sary's trust would make things harder but it wasn't catastrophic. She was running from something herself and probably still figured to use him. But if this pious bastard told her...

"Farraday's?" French said, and Grete knew it was coming. The rustler was broadening his jowls for a chuckle when a pistol appeared in Grete's hand. "You yap any more and you'll do it through gunsmoke."

Ben settled back with his eyes big as slop buckets. Idaho was caught with both arms on his saddlefork. Cook, bent from the waist, was braced to pick up an oven and French, after those lies, was not about to invite judgment. Only the girl showed animation. Her eyes, widely alert, had picked up the glint of the pistol, and a kind of pleased astonishment was breaking across the look of them.

Grete took a peek at Idaho. "Get the stock lined out for Animas."

Ben started a protest. Grete shook his head at him. "We're moving soon as cook gets hitched. Give the old gaffer a hand, kid."

He still had his gun on the rustler's middle when French, eyeing Sary, declared with a show of pained reluctance, "If Farraday's giving the orders—if you're not going through Stein's, I

39

may as well sever my arrangement with you now."

"Try it," Grete said, "and you'll have something else severed. I'm going to need every man we've got on this drive. Ben—" he called sharply, "you'll ride with Miz' Hollis; make sure you've got plenty of shells for that rifle. French, you'll ride with cook—go help him rustle those pans. Rest of this outfit will stay with the horses."

Idaho wheeled his bronc and rode off. Ben looked after him, sullenly scowling.

"You think I'm crippled?" French said, baring his teeth.

"You damn well will be if I have to tell you again."

There was no trouble that night.

They camped three hours in Animas Valley. Grete, pulling the gear off his horse, said abruptly, "You might as well swap that bed for a lantern, French. We're all going on nighthawk—catch up some fresh mounts."

There were too many wild horses on this part of the range to risk losing stock when close-herding would prevent it. Ben and French did a heap of grumbling. Sary climbed into her wagon without comment.

After a cold breakfast in the gray light of dawn, Farraday announced, "We'll be leaving these wagons. You can pack cook's supplies on some of those mares, but load the teams first and don't overdo it."

"What's the big idea?" Ben demanded, glowering.

"If you don't want your bones scattered over this prairie, quit jawing and get busy."

When Hollis didn't move—others had stiffened in their tracks to peer around at him—Grete put down the saddle he had just picked up. The quick wicked swing of his probing stare drove all expression from their faces. "We're in this together. You may as well make the best of it."

He stood a moment considering them, looking sharpest at Idaho, then rummaging French. These were the ones he could look to for trouble, French for his detention, Idaho for loss of face, for his aches and bruises and whatever had made him jump Grete in the first place.

"Like I said, we're leaving the wagons. Right where they are, pointed south. You and the kid, French, can help Patch pack—I'll cut out a few of the ruggedest mares for you. Idaho will cut out a score for Miz' Hollis who will hold them off to one side till I'm ready. You and Idaho, Ben, will get the rest headed north—"

"North!" Sary stared. "But I thought you said. . ."

"That was before I knew about French. We've got Curly Bill breathing down our necks now. When we don't show up for that bait Irv put out Bill's liable to start hunting. You can't outrun him. We're going to try to outfox him—you better hope that we do."

He was particularly watching French and the gunfighter but it was Ben had the hell in his neck this morning. "Cold grub, no sleep, now this," he snarled. "I think, by hell, you're fixin' to run off with the whole goddamn band!"

"Think what you want, just do what I tell you. And do it right away."

He watched them move off, aware that nothing had been settled, knowing what little chance there was really of succeeding in outfoxing the king of all foxes. Curly Bill knew this country like the palm of his hand. He'd have no trouble getting men. Tomorrow—next day at

41

the latest—at least one batch of ruffians would be prowling every route.

Sary touched Grete's elbow. Before she could get her thought into words, cook came up with an affronted look still riding the gullies of his ridgy cheeks. "Could be Bill's really after these broncs. If that's so we'd have a heap better chance if you wasn't mixed into this, bucko."

That was French's poison talking. Grete said bluntly, "You'd have no chance at all. They'd have you boxed—"

"But if we can't outrun them," Sary said, "why leave the wagons?"

"I'm not anxious to draw any map for Bill. We've got to move fast or we'll be caught in the open. We're gone ducks, believe me, if Bill's whole push comes down on us."

"What I said," the cook growled, "but if we got rid of you—"

"Patch, hush," Sary said, and Grete could see that she was following him. "You're hoping to lose our sign in the tracks of this wild stuff, or at any rate confuse them. But how will you keep them from spotting our dust?"

"Couldn't around here—that's why I want to get moving. He may not get after us before tomorrow or next day; he'll be expecting Irv to bring you over through Stein's. By then, if we're lucky, we could be out of his reach. We're going north into malpais—be no sign for him there. If we can mix him up here we might get through to Wilcox."

"That's good?" she said.

"It will be damned good if we can do it." Grete sighed. "He's got a front to keep up of being honest over there."

They looked at each other through a moment of silence. Impatience stirred her shoulders and color came guiltily to turn her away. She swung up onto the horse the kid had readied for her and rode off toward the mares left by Idaho. Grete watched the look of her against gray sky and, disquieted by the run of his thoughts, came around to find cook about set to go. The teams were packed and the mares, pawing restively, were nickering and squealing after the stock pushed ahead. "You're going to have trouble with that stud," Patch prophesied. "He ain't going to like havin' these mares split up."

"That's Idaho's problem, and Ben's," Grete said, darkly studying the slyness he found in French's stare. "If there's anything wearing shoes in this bunch, I want them pulled off—right away. We can't hide these horses in the tracks of wild stuff if we're putting down shoe sign. Kid, you stick with me," he said, and waved the others away.

He watched them pull out into the dust of the main bunch and all this while, on top of everything else, flight of time kept him worrying bitter thoughts of King Crotton. By pushing north into malpais he was adding more miles to the staggering distance already between them, miles he couldn't afford but would have to someway put under their hoofs if he would save these Shilohs for his ruckus with Swallowfork. If he could have dealt with French's buyers—but the man had no buyers. There was just Curly Bill who had never been known to pay for anything larger than a five cent glass of beer. Bill took what he wanted, stifling protests with bullets. The back trails were strewn with bones of damned fools.

"Packs are going to leave deeper sign," he told Barney Olds, pointing out the difference. "I want you to keep Miz' Hollis' bunch back, run them right over our tracks all the way. Been with her long?''

The kid shrugged, staring off into nothing until Grete said, "Queer kind of crew to fetch along with a horse drive . . . Reckon they worked for her husband and she didn't have the heart—''

Barney Olds said scornfully, "Tate wouldn't of give these scrubs the time of day!'' There was the heat of indignant anger in the look he slanched around him. "Never had no crew since I been with him; took every cent he could get his hands on to keep that sorry goddamn Ben—''

The kid quit, got red and glared resentfully at Grete. "I better git at my work,'' he said and walked at a horseman's saddle-cramped stride to a white-stockinged sorrel draped over its reins.

Farraday, swinging up, waved a hand and Sary started the held band of mares. If she hadn't hired this crew it must have been Ben. It was something to think about.

"Take over, kid.'' He nodded when Sary came up, and waved her on. "Make sure they're all barefoot,'' he said, and cut after her. "Where's Rip?'' he asked, pulling the dun in beside her.

She waved a hand. "On that bay, riding drag.''

"Takes most of his nourishment out of a bottle.'' At Grete's tightening lips she said defensively, "There wasn't much time. Ben did the best he could.''

There was a blend of things in this girl that troubled Farraday, considering her out of the corner of his eye; a wound-up tightness and hunger, some unsatisfied need, that could take them into dangerous places—as it was taking

44

them now. While he was still pondering this, grown irritable and dissatisfied, she said, "You'll not be at all surprised, I think, to learn you're driving stolen stock. You probably guessed as much when you named the terms. My acceptance told you how desperate I was."

"But not why," he said, liking her better for the admission.

"A woman's reputation is more brittle than a man's." She seemed to study this a while. "Don't think I'm crying after mine; what I've done I did with my eyes open. It's just. . ." Her voice turned small. "It would be intolerable to discover I had traded it for nothing."

He could understand that. He might be sharing the same intolerance if it turned out he'd thrown up a good thing without acquiring the ground he'd quit Crotton to file on. "You've got to go through with it."

I intended to," she nodded. Now she looked at him squarely. "It's not the law I'm afraid of—it's this crew. They've got it rigged to take over once we get to Arizona."

"It figures," Grete said, and scrubbed a hand along his jaw. "I'll take care of that." He flashed a sudden smile. "And who'll take care of me?"

She said in damned grim earnest, "One man I can probably handle. And it will surely be you if it looks like I'm headed for the short end of this stick."

FIVE

Grete put in a long day.

He kept flankers out—"Just like the goddamn Army!" cook testily grumbled—and
pushed the stock until even Sary protested.
"They'll be nothing but skin and bones!"

"But they'll still be ours," Grete reminded
her curtly, and rode on ahead again, making
sure their route led through plenty of horse sign.
The wild stock in this country kept the grass
chewed down to where there practically wasn't
any. It hurt him to see the pinched look of these
Shilohs but it would hurt a lot worse to have
Curly Bill grab them, and he kept reddened eyes
constantly prowling the horizons, searching for
riders or the glint of equipment, detouring
places that looked built for an ambush.

Around three o'clock he rode back past the
drag to make careful scout of the back trail.
Near as he could figure, since abandoning the
wagons, they had come about twenty miles,
twenty long and dusty miles which—considering this trek had originated in Texas and had
just stumbled out of the Jornada when he had
come up with it—was about all a man could look
to get out of them without he was willing to risk
grave losses. A cavalry patrol, even accom-
panied by wagons, could rock off a regular four
miles an hour, but cavalry was grain-fed,

toughened to it, and carried along by gaiting with fifteen-minute periods for rest. Twenty miles for this bunch was humping and Grete expected, before going into night camp, to chalk up another five.

He wanted, if he could, to get clean away from the region where French's boss would start hunting them. For hunt he would—Grete was positive of that. Curly Bill was a bold man, and deadly, a wastelands pirate in the shieldfronted shirt and rollbrim hat of the cowhand, a man who stole cattle by the entire herd and would go a long way to get hold of good horses which, in his kind of business, were an emphasized *must*.

Grete studied the spread-out folds of ground wave by wave without picking up any sign of pursuit. In all that vast stretch of earth and sky there was nothing to arouse suspicion except the lack of it. Bill's marauders, like Apaches, were seldom seen before they struck. Grete sat fifteen minutes inspecting various dust devils before putting them down to the antics of random air currents. And even then he was not satisfied. He would like to have had a glass on that country. Curly Bill around town might be a jovial sort of hail-fellow-well-met—an impression he deliberately cultivated; but found on a trail he was strictly business with no more compunctions than you'd find in a tiger. He raided army posts for remounts, killed prospectors and Mexican smugglers with impunity, stuck up stages, and occasionally sacked a bank. Not that you could prove it—Bill wasn't the kind to leave proof laying around.

Farraday wheeled the dun, more nagged by worry than he was willing to admit. While he lallygagged here the boys up ahead could be riding into a trap.

Not Idaho, he decided. That case-hardened

47

scrub was too wide between the horns to ride into anything he couldn't see through. Or was he?

Grete thought back to that business of yesterday, the way that cat-fingered son had jumped him, but Sary had probably been back of that; you couldn't tell what a galoot would do where a woman had got herself mixed into it. Packing a grass rope and forking a hull girthed front and flank, there was a look of Texas about the fellow; but there were Texas men in Bill's bunch too and this sidewinding saddle stiff might be one of them.

Farraday was about to swing into a lope when a piece of scuffed ground came under his eye, turning him back for a more careful look. His mouth tightened when he found what he'd seen to be exactly what he had figured it to be—the print of a shod hoof freshly made.

And there were others, equally fresh, up ahead, and more of them back of him like a trail of dropped sticks.

Farraday's eyes slimmed flintily. One of his own crew was leaving this sign. It wasn't scrabbled in with these barefoot tracks but laid on top of them. He said, *"That goddamn kid!"*

He dug hooks in the dun. But after the first quarter-mile the jarring pound of the pace began to shake holes through the blindness of temper and he let the horse drop back into a walk. Olds was only a boy with a boy's harum-scarum featherheadedness. . . .

But this wasn't the way he remembered the kid—a boy, yes, but one trying to fill the boots of a man. Barney would never have forgotten to pull the iron off his mount. *Was this deliberate then?*

What other notion could a man put upon it? Those tracks hadn't got here by accident.

Grete's half-shut eyes scrinched thoughtfully. He'd detached those mares from the rest of the band in an attempt to avoid what he now was confronted with. It had to be the kid; to have done as directed—to handle the mares at all—Barney Olds would have had to keep them ahead of him. It had to be the kid's horse.

Staring after that curtain of shimmering dust, Grete was sure no outsider could be putting down tracks between himself and those mares. There was, right here, no place a strange rider could hide—he would have to be in sight of either Grete or Barney Olds.

Hating this, Farraday looked around again but there wasn't a brush patch larger than a pig, no concealment at all for a man on a horse. Or for a riderless horse. Sick with revulsion, outraged, furious, Grete put the gelding into a run. This wasn't a chore that putting off would take care of it. It was a question of survival and he had to act for all of them.

A hundred yards short of the drag he pulled rein to loosen and resettle the big gun at his hip. A man didn't like to throw down on a kid but a small snake could kill you just as certain as a big one, and this was treachery. On second thought he withdrew the gun and rode with it cocked across the pommel of his saddle.

Through the dust he caught blurred glimpses of the mares and now he saw the rider, hunched over and nursing the cant of a rifle. Holding the dun to a walk he put him into their tracks and the gelding's longer stride began to overhaul Olds. It wasn't being heard Grete was scared of but of the kid twisting around and, suddenly discovering him, being stampeded into clawing for his trigger. It could happen that way.

But it didn't. The mares had just rimmed

the brow of a rock-strewn ridge when something turned the fellow and their glances briefly locked across that gray powdery swirl of churned-up dust. There wasn't fifty feet between them. Both men were startled. It would have been difficult to say which was the more surprised, French or Farraday. French whipped up the rifle. Flame popped out of its mouth like a snake's tongue. A mushroom of smoke swirled against the dust. Flame came out of it and, finally, the racket.

The fool was firing too fast, banking on luck or sheer speed to get the job done. Farraday's eyes were polished granite. Without flurry or fluster he got the man in his sights and squeezed off one shot. The sudden plunging whirl of French's horse saved the man, yet even so the slug smashed into him, spilling him, screaming, out of the saddle.

Grete saw the mares tearing off like a twister, the shapes of spurring riders plummeting toward him from two directions, but the core of his attention remained unwaveringly on French who still had hold of his mount by one rein and was trying to get onto his feet against the tug of it. The man had lost his rifle but he still had a pistol and Grete expected him to go for it.

The riders pounded up and Ben Hollis, shouting furiously, demanded to be told what Farraday thought he was trying to pull off here. Grete saw Sary and the kid and back of them another man staring with big eyes while his yellow snags of teeth worried the cork out of a bottle.

"Irv took first shot," Grete said. "Let him explain it."

French was white-faced above the blood on his shirt and was shaking like a dog caught out in a blue norther. He said in a quavery outraged voice, "I never even fired at all!"

Grete had started to shove the pistol back in his holster but now, scanning their faces, changed his mind and kept hold of it. "Maybe," he said scornfully, "I just imagined the whole thing."

French fumbled the gun from his hip and with an affronted look held it out to the girl. Sary held up the barrel and sniffed and shook her head, too shocked to peak.

"Not that," Grete said. "He was using a rifle."

They all looked at French's horse. "What rifle?" Ben said.

"It's around here somewhere. He must have let go of it when he went out of the saddle."

Ben, the kid helping, scuffed around in the dust, his thoughts very plain when he gave over to stand peering up at Grete blackly. "Why would he shoot at you?"

Sary got down, still holding French's pistol, and went over to the man, telling the kid to fetch water—"and Rip's bottle," she added.

But Ben wasn't leaving it there. "Why would he shoot at you, Farraday? If you've anything to say you'd better get at it."

Grete said in cold contempt, "I caught him leaving sign for his friends. When he saw I was onto him he grabbed up that rifle."

"What kind of sign?" Idaho asked, face expressionless.

Farraday waved his left hand. "Look around."

Idaho, considering him, presently nodded, "Kid, take a look," he said. Sary got through with her first aid on French and gave back what was left in the bottle to its owner. The fellow held it up to the light, took a swig and drove

51

home the cork. The kid, who had been prowling wit¹ a plain and growing bewilderment, now looked past the sneering Ben to say to Grete, "What kind of sign?"

"Shod hoofs," Grete said, tightening his grip on the pistol.

The kid shook his head. "You better show me where."

Cold warning slapped through Grete like a hatpin, narrowing his stare, touching off all the alarms he had so carefully buried in a growing disquiet. He said through the frozen mask of his fears, "You'd better look, Sary. Go back a ways where they haven't boogered up the ground."

Her glance was uncomfortably remindful of the searching look he had got from the gunfighter but she moved away, following Olds without comment. Ben's hateful stare, grown rank with distrust, unwinkingly watched through the layers of silence that were like walls of stone going up around Farraday.

Grete said, "Somebody better keep an eye on those Shilohs."

"Patch is out there. So is Frijoles." Idaho, turning his horse, sat apart with an ox-like patience while they waited for the girl and Barney Olds to return. The fellow with the bottle rasped beard-stubbled cheeks had peered around with bleary eyes that seemed to have a hard time focusing. His stomach rumbled and a belch came out of him and French crawled into his saddle with a groan.

"How bad is it, Irv?" That was Ben. His eyes watched Farraday with the steadiness of a cat's.

"I'll live through it," French muttered; and then Sary was back with her glance like two holes hacked through winter ice.

Farraday knew without asking she hadn't

52

found anything. "You didn't go far enough."

Ben's eyes were ugly. "If there was tracks she'd of found them."

This appeared to be in line with what the rest of them were thinking. "Pick up the feet of his horse," Grete said doggedly.

French sneered when she came over but offered no objections. Sary lifted the animal's feet one by one, displaying its hoofs. Grete, recalling his earlier conviction, said, "Try Barney's," but the result was the same. The hoofs of both horses showed where nails had been pulled but there were no shoes in evidence.

Rip took another gurgling snort from his bottle, rammed the butt of it down the side of his coat and, imaging it safe in his pocket, let go. The bottle shattered on a stone, its trickle of whisky staining the dirt. He hiccuped and said with a drunk's owlish gravity: "How unsearchable are His judgments, how inscrutable His ways."

Nobody laughed. They were all watching Grete and he reckoned by their looks he might as well argue with the shadow of death as try to carry this business any further. "Let's get this drive moving." He waved them away with the barrel of his pistol. "We've got another four miles to put under our belts and we'll do it if we have to trail half the night!"

Ben wanted to make something more of the shooting but, finding no encouragement, rode after the others.

"Sary—" Grete called, but she paid no attention. French went off with the rest of them but the kid, after a bit, swung around and came back. He looked uncertain, a little worried. "If you want to crawl my frame. . ."

"Forget it," Grete said, his bleak stare following Sary.

But the kid wasn't built that way. "If I'd stayed back here like you told me—"

"Let's get these mares moving. What's done is done. Crying over spilled milk ain't going to butter no parsnips."

The kid pulled his mouth together but the knowledge of his part in what had happened back there was a thing his conscience couldn't let be, even if the boss did choose to ignore it. He kept covertly eyeing the granite look of Grete's face and, after they'd gone about a quarter-mile, blurted, "I'd be glad to go back an' look again for that rifle."

Farraday glanced at him sharply, then shrugged. "Suit yourself."

He heard the kid turn his horse, fading away in the dust which, back here, was like riding through a bowlful of smoke. These mares had been on the trail long enough that a man didn't have to keep taking off after one. They'd have followed the stallion anyway. Normally the only problem a crew would have on a drive like this was keeping the boss horse headed where you wanted the band to go. The big problems here were strickly two-legged ones. The composition of the crew. The proximity of outlaws.

Farraday knew Ben hadn't half looked for that rifle. He couldn't see that it would make any great amount of difference whether Barney came back with the gun or not; be pretty hard now to tie it to French. His mount's shoes were likely tucked away in Irv's pockets. He'd been pretty damned cute any way you wanted to look at it.

Grete was scowling at the hair between the dun's ears, still thinking about it, when Idaho, coming up through the dust, cut his horse in beside him. "Where you figurin' to camp?"

"Don't know," Grete said. "We've got malpais ahead. I'd like—"

"How far ahead?"

Grete shrugged again.

"We ought to hole up while we can see what the chances are."

Farraday scowled at him. "Pick your own place," he said. "I figure you and me have got no fuss that can't wait."

"My notion, too." Staring at Grete, Idaho seemed to be trying to make up his mind to something. He finally brought out four shoes from the slicker strapped back of his cantle. "I've got nails if you need 'em."

Grete took the shoes and looked a long while at the barred one. Then his glance bit at Idaho. "How'd you get them?"

Idaho showed a cruel flash of teeth. "That bar was a giveaway if anyone went back."

"Why didn't he just drop them?"

"And have somebody see him doin' it? We've talked before. If anything busted I'd be the one wigglin' around on the hot spot."

"So you slip them to me."

Idaho's raw-red cheeks showed contempt. He kicked steel at his horse and rode off toward the front again. With the iron in his hand Grete stared after him, wondering. This could be on the level or it could be another peg they hoped to drive in his coffin.

The kid had the rifle when he presently caught up. There was excitement in his stare and an on-the-prod set to the forward hunch of his shoulders. "All right," Grete said, "you've seen it. Now take it off somewhere and lose it."

Barney Olds looked astonished. He opened his mouth, halfway angry.

"If you're found packing two saddle guns *and* these plates," Farraday said, "you'll be grub for a coyote before you're many hours older." He held out the shoes that had been pulled from French's horse.

Barney's eyes goggled.

"Take them," Grete told him. "Soon's you find a bush that looks tall enough to hide in, get them on your bronc and start laying down tracks."

The kid was eyeing him queerly. "They won't fit this mare—"

"They'll stay on her long enough to get the job done if you're careful. I want a trail laid off toward those mountains. There's tracks all over this dirt around here. Pick you out a good batch and leave that shod sign on top of them. Keep going until you're riding on rock. Pull these shoes and leave the rifle. We'll be somewhere off there—" Farraday pointed north. "Think you can handle it?"

"You're goddamn right!"

SIX

Pushing the drag through the miles-long shadows bent down from the mauve and cobalt shapes of the mountains, Grete, coming onto the first jumble of lava rock, derived a mordant sort of humor from the thought of Bill's robbers gustily tracking French's plates into nowhere. It made an enticing picture but he did not permit himself to be fooled into thinking this ruse would rid them of danger. It would buy them a little time perhaps and maybe siphon off some of that kill-crazy crowd into places Grete had no intention of going, but it would not get them scot-free into Willcox. Bill was too crafty for anything like that; portions of his gang would already have been sent to close off every outlet into the west.

In his mind now, like the *segundo* he had been, Grete traced the probabilities to their inevitable conclusions. Somewhere ahead this drive would run into trouble; he was as certain of this as he was of Ben's enmity. Just why Hollis should hate him he could not quite fathom but he had no doubt at all concerning the inevitability of gunsmoke.

In a way he could almost welcome this for it would shake down the crew and show him what he had to work with. Crotton's bunch were as solidly rugged as anything Bill was like to throw against them and intrenched, besides, in a tradition of past victories. Crotton's empire was no greater than his ability to hold it and he would know that once the bars came down every neighbor and pushed-out squatter would throw their weight against him. Thus Grete could see in the imminent prospect of bracing a fragment of Bill's owlhoot legion a very real value to the plans he had shaped; but there was also grave danger. This crew might run out on him. They might not be willing to defend horses with their lives. They might not be able to, and they might—it was certainly possible—use the confusion of any conflict to put a bullet through his back.

These were things he had to think about.

He was still thinking about them without having reached any useful conclusions when he came at early dusk upon the camp to discover Idaho, with folded arms, sardonically eyeing a pair of angry-faced strangers. "There's the boss," Idaho nodded. "Dump your troubles on him."

"What's gnawing you?" Grete said, staring down at the pair.

Both were chunky-built men, heavily armed and cocked for killing. There was enough facial resemblance for Grete to mark the pair as brothers. Each had a fist belligerently spread within short reach of a pistol. The younger of the two, tipping up his scrinched face, threw his words at Grete in a voice that gave notice to nothing but rage. "You fellers have got your guts, by grab!"

"What's the rub?"

"We don't want no outside horse stock in here. We're ranchin' this valley!"

Farraday said reasonably, "We're heading for the pass. I'll be out of—"

58

"You're gettin' out right now! Get then animals turned around! You're goin' back where you came from!"

The man was riled enough to die for it. Grete, considering him solemnly, shook his head. "That's not hardly possible, mister. We'll be gone in the morning—"

"I don't doubt that! And with half our stock! I know you damn Texicans! By grab, I tell you right now—"

"You ain't tellin' nobody, Fatso." Idaho had a gun in his fist and no hold on the hammer but the tension of his thumb.

"Wait a minute," Grete said. They could do it this way and likely make it stick, but not for long. The mares needed rest, they had to have grass and water. If he ran this wild-eyed pair off now they'd be back before morning, and probably with help. There was a better way. He made himself smile. "Have you looked over our stock?" he asked conversationally.

The older man nodded. "You've got some good blood there. We don't like to be so feisty mean but we're in horses ourselfs and we don't aim—"

"You won't lose any stock to us," Grete cut in. "As a matter of fact, if you'll privilege us with a stake of grass and water and room for these mares to rest up a few hours, you can have your pick of any pair takes your fancy."

Sary had come up with Ben while they were talking but Grete didn't look to see how she was taking this. He didn't look at Idaho, either, but prayed like hell the pistoleer would string along, at least to the extent of keeping his mouth shut.

Idaho did, but Ben Hollis chucked in his two and one half cents worth. "Over my dead body!" he snarled, thrusting himself forward

59

like an overgrown lout of a kid in front of company.

Farraday could cheerfully have brained the sonofabitch. Instead, he ignored him, appraising the older brother's curious stare, observing the younger brother twisting about for another look at the mares he'd come in with which Rip was chousing off now toward where Frijoles and cook were loose-herding the rest of them.

The older man said, "We'd like to be neighborly. . ."

"We'll undertake to ride herd on them," Grete smiled persuasively, noting the curl of Idaho's lip. "I can keep the whole crew at it if that'll ease your mind any. We'll take them over to the seep and bed them down or up into that stand of blackjack just this side of the pass if you'd like that better."

Idaho turned away with a snort and got onto his horse and rode after Rip.

"What's the name of this place?" Sary asked, and the younger brother came around to stare at her.

Grete said, "Happy Valley," and found the older man giving him a sharper scrutiny.

"You've been here before."

"Worked cattle all through this country," Grete nodded.

The younger one said, "If they'll ride herd on their stock I vote we take 'em up on it. There's a sorrel filly in that bunch would suit me fine."

Ben's face flushed darkly for the fellow was looking at Sary when he said it. Grete was surprised to discover resentment in himself; this piled flesh fuel on the rage smoldering in him. But he kept it off his face. "If that's all right with you," he said to the other one, "go ahead and make your pick. I want to get these mares to water.''

The older brother didn't like being rushed. You could see it. He paid no attention at all to the girl but kept looking around at Ben. Now he said, "You got the right to do what you want with these horses?''

"I've got the right of a trail boss and a half interest on top of that.''

The bold eyes of the younger one kept ogling Sary with an open lust that was hard to take. Ben caught hold of her arm and towed her away and the older one said, "We'll want bills of sale for them.''

"In the morning," Grete nodded.

"We'll make our pick now.''

They rode over to where the band was being held and Grete was starting to break a lantern from a pack when the older one said, "You've got to take them past the ranch. We've got chutes. We'll pick 'em there.''

Just short of full dark they sighted the buildings. There was a horse trap and chutes and three stout corrals made of blackjack oak, one of them a round one with a post set in its center. The two brothers went on ahead to make ready. Sary came up to Farraday then. "I hope you know what you're doing," she said.

"We'll have trouble enough without fighting them. How's French?''

"For a hardcase," she said, "you're not much of a shot.''

"You give him back his pistol?''

He couldn't catch her expression in the failing light but could tell by the stiffening set of her shoulders it had been a fool thing to ask. He was disgruntled to find himself saying, "Been no point in me trying to kill him after he shot off his mouth.''

"I didn't think so, either."

They rode a few strides before that one caught up with him. She knew when it did by the sharp look he gave her. She said, "What have you done with Barney Olds?"

He was riled enough then to ignore her completely. He was minded to bad enough. Instead he said curtly: "You're welcome to ride back and look if you want."

It was childish, he reckoned. She had no reason to trust him. And why the hell should he give a damn! He discovered he did and that hacked him still more. He spun the gelding away from her.

They'd got a light at the chutes and Ben's handpicked crew was getting the stock strung out toward the wing. The brothers had hung lanterns onto posts above the squeeze and now were scrambling up. If they worked help there wasn't any in evidence. A dozen horses in the trap were sending quips at the mares but the latter had caught the smell of water and were letting the crew know it, kicking and biting, raising general hell. Idaho caught one's rump with a rope's end. "Send 'em through!" one of the brothers yelled.

Ben and Frijoles up at the front got them started. They had to crowd them against the fence and even then they kept trying to break around, so wild had they become. Grete gave Rip and Idaho a hand. Then Sary was calling, "They'll founder if you let them get at that water!"

"Get over by the springs," Farraday yelled, "and snap your fish at them." He looked around for Idaho. "Where's French?" he growled.

"Said there was springs at the pass and grass where we could hold 'em. I sent him on with cook."

A big roan broke out of the bunch and Grete went after her but the dun was too weary; she got off into the dark before Crete could make his throw. He rethonged the rope to the fork of his saddle, looked around once again, and headed for the springs to give Sary a hand with the mares as they came larruping up after clearing the chute. "Where's the stud?" he asked.

"Gone ahead with Patch." She heard Grete swear. She said, "He's tractable enough; you needn't worry about him."

Grete wasn't. It was French and the man's proximity to a fast and valuable means of transportation that made him swing down and pull her out of the saddle. "Use mine," he growled and, catching hold of her reins, was up and slapping the filly into a run before Sary realized what he was up to.

As he'd suspected, this mount, though gaunted from travel and the day's lack of water, had a lot more left in her than the dun he'd got off of. He put her into a lope and overtook one of the mares which, having been turned from the springs, was following her nose into the damp air from the pass.

Riding through oak brush, avoiding thickets of mesquite, he soon sighted Patch's fire off ahead through the night. In the last hundred yards he reined down to a walk, seeing the black shapes of the men among the thirsty stock which had got there ahead of him. Cook was fighting the mares away from water while French eased them into it three or four at a crack, hardly giving them time to wet their muzzles before whacking them out of it to make room for others. Both men had their hands full. Neither of them spoke though he caught French several times eyeing him covertly. Patch said presently, when the worst of it eased off, "If you

an' Irv can handle this now I'll try to get some
kind of a bait throwed together."

"Go ahead," Grete said, and looked around
for the stud. The big Steeldust, with several of
the mares, was off to one side cropping at the
standing feed which was here mostly salt grass
and grama. The horse for some reason appeared
to be nervous, looking up and around every
couple of mouthfuls. Excited by all this
chousing of the mares, probably. "I know,"
Grete told French, "you're busting to cut loose
of this. Just don't try it if you crave to stay
healthy."

They watered the latest arrivals and hazed
them off toward the others. French keeping his
mouth shut. Cook had already got the packs off
one pair of the work teams and now, with
French helping, Grete unloaded the other and
got to work on the mares. The stud, he noticed,
still continued to seem uneasy, frequently
quitting the grass to prowl around with his head
up, occasionally biting at a mare. Another batch
came in whickering and French chased them
away from the water before they could get
enough to cause any trouble. Farraday made a
rough count, deciding most of them were here.
Coffee smell came from the direction of the fire,
and he was twisting around to suggest to
French they go try some when the stallion
sharply bugled.

"Crew's comin'," cook grumbled, "an' I
ain't got the damn stew het up yet. If you
wanta—"

But Grete was suddenly discovering French
had given him the slip. He'd got completely out
of sight and Farraday, wheeling around,
couldn't find the stallion, either. He plunged
into the oaks, hearing the crew plainly now and

64

the crackle of brush in the black somewhere ahead of him. If French got away everything they'd done was useless.

Back toward the fire he could hear the growl of Idaho's voice, the chinging of spur rowels, the slither of bit chains. He reached down, taking off his own spurs, which he wrapped in his neckerchief and thrust inside the front of his shirt while he listened, rummaging the night with his stare. Someplace to the left of him, deeper into the oaks, brush snapped again and a horse blew out a gusty breath and Grete, with nerves pulled tight as fiddle strings, lifted the pistol off his hip and went storming into the branch-black gloom.

Too late he glimpsed the solider dark of a man's crouched shape lunging erect in his path, the in-swinging blur of an enlargening arm that he could not duck and could not stop short of. The world exploded inside his head, all falling lights, and he went spiralling down into a crackle of oak leavs and bent-over grass.

It was the shot pulled him out of it, its sound near enough to strike physically against him. He got a hand braced and pushed his chest off the ground, hearing the echoes break and run and, farther back, the shouts like dim whispers floating through the pound of feet.

He saw the grotesque dance of monstrous shadows and staggered up out of the clinging mists into a kaleidoscope whirl of brush, shapes, and faces. Blinding light fell over him and something pushed at his fist and something else tugged his memory; then the light fell away and became a held-up lantern, and a solidness directly in front of him was the accusing look of Ben Hollis. There was a ring of faces peering over Ben's shoulder and a waiting sort of stillness which was indescribably ugly.

"Well," Hollis prodded, "what have you got to say for yourself?"

Grete shook his head, trying to clear away the grogginess. He started to shove the girl's brother-in-law aside and something came hard against his stomach.

Glancing down he saw the cocked gun in Ben's fist and, under it, the twisted shape sprawled between them. French still looked like a character out of Scripture—and just about as dead.

SEVEN

"What happened?" Sary called, pushing a way through the ring of faces. Her own turned gray as wood ash when she discovered Irv French with a hole through his head.

"What does it look like?" Ben said, sneering. "He's already tried once. This time he got the job done!"

"Are you trying to say Farraday. . .?"

"Here's his gun," Ben said. "I just took it away from him."

She must have shown disbelief because Idaho said, "I seen that much." A couple more of them nodded. Sary took the pistol and shook out four cartridges; the other shell stuck and showed the mark of the hammer. She tipped up the barrel and fetched the muzzle to her chin. "Look at Ben's," Grete said when he saw the way she eyed him.

Hollis, with a scornful laugh, passed over his gun without any argument, but could not forebear saying, "*I* got nothing to hide."

Sary took the gun—a Schofield Smith & Wesson chambered for the .45 caliber center-fire cartridge—and, without touching the barrel-latch, moved it past her nose. Her eyes looked at Crete without any expression but he was willing to gamble it had not been fired. Still carrying Farraday's unloaded Colt and its cartridges in her left hand she came around Rip and the Mexican to stop beside Grete, saying, "It wasn't Ben's pistol."

Farraday stared at the man for a moment, cursing himself for underestimating Hollis. The fellow might have the lip of a muley cow and no more grit than you would find in a rabbit, but there wasn't anything wrong with the wheels in his think-box. He was telling the others:

"I've been suspicious of this ranny right from the start. All that yap about tracks! Sary and I both looked. It seemed plain enough when neither one of us found 'em it was just something he'd cooked up to excuse jumping French."

Glancing around he said grimly, "The real point of that business only hit me a few minutes ago. If he could leave a few tracks and then match them with plates found in Irv's duffle he'd have a pretty good case—particular if French was in no position to disprove it. I knew then he'd try again.

"When I seen Irv duck into these oaks just now, and Farraday ramming into them after him. I fed the hooks to my bronc and cut over, figuring to head them. But I cut over too far. I was just swinging back when I heard the shot."

He said bitterly, "I didn't see him kill Irv. But the light from your lanterns showed where Irv was. I found Farraday standing over him—smoke still coming out of that Colt gun. I ran up and wrassled it away from him."

Farraday, reaching over, took Ben's gun from Sary's hand as casually as though he were about to sniff its barrel. He made sure, instead, the patent barrel-latch was locked and, smiling coldly at Hollis, slipped a finger around the trigger. "Very plausible," he said, "but what's it all about? I haven't denied killing French. As

68

for those tracks—" he glanced at Sary, "they were there if you'd wanted to find them. Olds, when he gets back, can tell you all about it."

"Olds!" Hollis blurted, and threw a wild look about him.

"The kid," Grete said patiently. "Barney Olds—hadn't you missed him? French slipped the plates to Idaho. I gave them to Barney to put on his horse—along with the rifle which the kid also found, and told him to put down a trail into the mountains. Whatever Irv may have been up to isn't like to come off quite the way it was planned."

They all caught the black look Hollis stabbed at the gunfighter. Idaho, loosening bony shoulders, ignored him, heading back for the fire. "Gee-rusalem!" Rip said, and felt around for his bottle.

Hollis bared his teeth; but after looking at his Schofield casually balanced in Farraday's fist he shut his face—as someone said afterward "hard enough to bust his nut-crackers."

Sary said, "What are you going to do about . . . that?"

Grete looked down at French. "I guess," he said, not without an edge of malice, "we'll let Mr. Hollis take care of Irv. Rest of you better go hang on the nose bag. In case you've forgot, we've got stock to ride herd on."

Sary, as they moved back toward the grub, returned Grete's pistol and cartridges. He gave her Ben's Schofield. "A poor weapon to be caught with in this kind of country. It sure excells at unloading—spills empties and lives ones all over your lap, but it sure don't get along good with this dust. Cavalry had to get rid of them." He pulled his stare from the swell of her shirt and brought his mind bitterly to the business in hand. "Case you're wondering about those fillies. . ."

Her head came around. "But I thought you traded—"

"I sold those jaspers a bill of goods. We had to find grass and we had to have water. Happens all the water in this country's right here; those springs that pair have squatted on, this seep and a hole at the other side of the pass." He didn't know why he was bothering to explain this.

She said after a moment, "Why didn't you just plug them the way you did French? It'll come to that, won't it?"

"We might have lost some of the crew. They was set for it then." He punched the empty out of the Colt's cylinder and reloaded, thrusting the gun back into its holster. "If they've got to be shot I'll drop them where it won't matter."

They went the rest of the way in silence. But as they came up to the fire she said to him quietly, "You're tough and pretty ruthless but you're not quite the bastard you make yourself out to be."

She turned away, picking up a cup and tin plate, and set about the business of getting them filled. He thought angrily, staring after her: *Now where did she come up with that idea?* and twisted his jaw to look across the fire at Idaho. He hadn't yet got it smoothed out in his head what the gunfighter's stake in this deal added up to. He remembered Ben's baleful look after mention of French's plates, and cursed impotently under his breath. These were the men he was going to have to make his fight with and he had better weigh them careful.

He got a layout of tools for himself from cook's box and bent over the kettle, afterwards forking a couple of biscuits from the oven and dumping a splash of black coffee into one of the battered tin cups. This was just about the kind of crew a guy would pick if he was fixing to make off with a fortune in horses. It was hard, nevertheless, to imagine Ben killing French for the sake of the hole he must have reckoned the man's death would put Farraday into. It had come near enough doing it, Grete thought, suddenly sweating.

A galoot who would go that far to gain his ends was nobody to stamp your foot and yell *boo* at. It was a sobering thought. With his mouth full of stew he turned it over, glimpsing one other thing. Sary had said she was afraid of this crew, yet Ben had put it together. She had also claimed they were after her horses, but again you were forced to come back to Ben Hollis. If a man covered his dead brother's horses, might he not also lust after that brother's comely wife?

One by one the men swabbed out their plates and went off to the *caballada*. Farraday dug out the makings and patched up a smoke, trying to trace out the probable succession of events by which Ben might hope to gain control of this stock. But he remained too aware of Sary's proximity to get very far with any serious thinking.

He got up, grinding out the butt of his cigarette, and tossed his tableware into the wreck pan. Biggest problem right now centered around Curly Bill. That false trail the kid was laying might keep Bill himself off their necks, or it might not. But this was the best Grete could look for. The moment that swarthy outlaw decided the horses weren't coming through Stein's he'd have moved to seal off every trail they might use and then, with what was left of his men, he'd have set out to find them.

Grete snaked a fresh mount from the cavvy

under rope off to one side at the left of the fire. You couldn't turn geldings in with mares, particularly when there was a stallion around. It was remarkable when you stopped to think of it that Steeldust behaved as well as he did. Someone had obviously spent a lot of time with him. Barney, probably—he seemed to have a knack with stock. French had a way with stock too, Grete remembered, and irascibly hoped his faith in the kid would prove better justified than his snap judgment of Hollis.

It was Idaho that Grete couldn't figure. Considering the pounding that lay between them the gunfighter's present cooperative attitude looked phony as anything Grete had come up against. Had Idaho swallowed his feelings or was he only dissembling? By every standard the man should be itching to take a fall out of Grete to recover the prestige Grete's fists had drubbed out of him. That thing of him coming up with French's plates still had Grete going around in circles. Or maybe it was lack of rest that made his head hurt.

He considered the mares and found the bulk of them grazing. Stars glimmered like jewels in the black night above them. There was no wind. The moon, in its last quarter, had not yet come up. A rider drifted out of the dark motte of trees with a soft *"Quien es?"*

"Farraday," Grete said. "Everything quiet?"

The Mexican shrugged. *"Poco bueno."*

"Where's Idaho?"

Frijoles pointed. "Far side, I sink."

"Slip back and catch a few winks." Farraday rode on. He was so exhausted he could hardly keep his eyes open. He yawned prodigiously. Next horseman he encountered was Rip. He sent the man in. Off somewhere above

72

the pass a coyote irritably yammered, and a picture came up in Grete's mind of the way Ben had looked when the younger of those two blockheads had made his crack about a "sorrel filly." Stifling a yawn he saw the forward-hunched gauntness of Idaho drift out of the gloom.

"Damn funny thing," the gunfighter said, "we ain't seen more of them broncs those two rannies is supposed to be raisin'. I run off one stray and Rip choused a couple. Way that pair acted, a feller would think these goddamn rocks was bulgin' with stock."

"Range ain't fenced," Grete said without giving much thought to the matter. "God, but I'm tired!" He yawned again, allowing the horse to carry him away from the gunfighter. Then he skreaked round to call, "I sent Rip and Frijoles back to the fire to catch some sleep."

He didn't know if Idaho heard him or not. He guessed it didn't make any hell of a lot of difference. He hadn't forgot what he was doing here. His mind never strayed far from Crotton. It never strayed very far away from Sary either, and this tendency he despised as an indicated soft streak in a purpose that was otherwise as hard as rage could make it.

Perhaps he drowsed. It looked like some of the mares had gone to sleep on their feet. Something got through to him, rousing him enough to pull the chin off his chest. Sary's voice said out of the darkness, "You'd better get off that horse before you fall off."

"I'm all right," Grete muttered.

"That's pure stubbornness talking. This crew can't take the punishment you're giving it—a man's got to rest. Listen to me, Grete—"

"I'm awright," he snarled, angered.

"You're not all right and neither are the rest

of them. You don't have to kill yourselves nursing this stock. The stud will take care of . . . Anyway, I haven't seen any—have you?"

Farraday knuckled his eyes, trying to grind the sleep out of them, dragging his hands down across the rasp of unshaved cheeks. "Have I what?"

"Seen any loose stock. For horse ranchers that pair don't seem to have many horses. I've got a feeling," she said darkly, "there's something wrong here someplace."

Grete stared at her blearily. The flutter of her words flapping round inside his head vaguely stirred something touched by Idaho when the man had spoken to him earlier; but he couldn't seem to get his thoughts scraped together.

"You don't know that pair, do you?" Sary's voice prodded him.

"How the hell," he said irrelevantly, "does that one-eyed wooden-legged cook stick a saddle?"

"He's got a cut-off rifle scabbard rigged for a stirrup. Here—" she passed her water bag to him. "Splash some of that on your face and pay attention."

He noticed while he was doing this the nervous way she kept peering off into the dark. He sleeved his cheeks and gave her back the corked bag. "Supposing," she said, "someone *had* started a ranch here. That pair we saw don't have to be the ranchers. They could be somebody Curly Bill—"

"By God!" he said, suddenly coming wide awake.

"They could have been here to hold up this drive. One of them even now might be riding—"

"I can damn soon find out!" he said, thinking how goddamn stupid he'd been. He

74

gave her a kind of wondering look, for the first time actually considering this woman.

She smiled at him oddly with her head tipped back so that starlight showed the faint shine of her teeth. "Perhaps we've both," she said softly, "been thinking things we've had no right to." They stared a moment longer. Impulsively she put out a hand and he took it, feeling a confusion of warmth rush all through him.

Then, recalling his plans, he turned loose of her, anger lashing the sick shame that unaccountably laid hold of him. Was he a child to be swayed by the swish of a skirt!

Swearing under his breath he sent the horse curvetting away, wheeling its head toward the deep stain of trees that twenty yards out cut across the trail to hide the ranch's distant buildings.

The horse hadn't hardly got into its stride before Grete saw the tall blackness squarely set across his path. He pulled up with his nerves and his fears jerking at him. He caught the pale glint of gun steel and the motionless legs of a horse plain below it; all else was obscure against the smother of trees.

There was nothing obscure about Idaho's voice. "You won't be needin' no woman when you're stone-cold dead!"

EIGHT

While Farraday, growing wilder and angrier, was trying to catch up with the full import of this, a second blotch walked its horse out of the shadows and, coming up on Grete's far side, revealed the scowling rage-roughened cheeks of Ben Hollis. But it was the gunfighter Farraday continued to watch while the tone of those echoing words carried alarm through every nerve in his body.

He wrapped both hands over the pommel of his saddle. "So you've patched up your fences," he said at last, gruffly.

"Never mind about that!" Idaho's voice held the twang of stretched wire. "Keep away from her—hear?"

Farraday pressed his mouth together and something about this wicked calm seemed almost beyond bearing. "I hear you," Grete said; and Hollis, breathing raggedly, suddenly backed his horse away from them.

Although expecting trouble and braced for it ever since he'd hooked on with this drive, Farraday abruptly was left without speech. The gunfighter's glance, aroused as the stalking hunger of a tiger left him nothing to get behind. Looking into that unwinking gaze it suddenly came over Grete that neither horses nor any damage which could have stemmed from the beating he had given the man was behind this. Loss of face at Grete's hands had nothing to do with the gunfighter's fury. Farraday was appalled.

And yet, inexplicably mixed with his revulsion and shock, was a chastening humility, a reaching out, almost a compassion for this gaunt ox of a man, this hardcase spawned of chaparral and gunsmoke—in some weird way a kind of affinity. Something of this may have crept through his tone. "All right," he said, "you can back off now. You've got no quarrel with me."

But the man, too wound up, couldn't ease off the hook. His feelings were too powerful, too ravaged by suspicion and the ugly visions bred of it, to accept any easy assurance. Knowing what Grete had been to Crotton's brawling empire, he read into Farraday's tame reaction something which he could not brook. He had no faith in Grete's sincerity. It was too alien, too contrary to personal experience.

Grete, sensing this, gauging the futility of attempting to convince the man, picked up his reins. "When I go hungering after a petticoat—"

"Never mind! You been warned. Get this straight," Idaho growled harshly. "Long as your actions stay in line with her best interests I'll back your play. When they don't I'm comin' after you."

Farraday reined his horse about, too bitterly furious to risk further words.

No light showed in the log house of the brothers, but this was a country that went early to bed. In the east the great orange disc of the moon was pushing its face above the black steeps of Knight Mountain, bathing in leprous ochers the roundabout knobs and ridges.

He paused after a bit for a glance at his back trail, peering into the dark of trees, the deception of shadow patches, remembering Ben who might not be above taking his goose any way he could catch him. But he saw nothing which alarmed him and presently went on, walking the horse, hand by the butt of his holstered pistol.

He reckoned he'd better get rid of that gunfighter. Sooner or later the man would breed trouble. Idaho wouldn't like the Swallowfork end of this. He would consider that Grete had lied to the girl, bent the truth inexcusably, cheating her; he might force a showdown Grete wasn't ready for.

This made Grete shake his head. Getting rid of the man wasn't in the cards. When they came up against Crotton Grete would need every one of them. Regardless of that, Grete's hands were tied. Idaho was in deadly earnest about Sary; whether or not he had any chance in that quarter, the gunfighter's interest in the girl would never permit Grete to send him packing; and Farraday, in this brew he had cooking, couldn't afford to be laughed at or ignored. He might just as well pitch in his hand as to issue an order he couldn't make stick. The fellow would never let it come to fists again.

Anger came up in Grete's throat so thick it choked him. But he couldn't find any way around his dilemma. He didn't have to grab any gypsy's fist to know he'd wedged himself between a rock and a hard place.

He paused again, halfway down, to take a feel of the wind. There was precious little blowing but it made him do some shifting to come onto the flat where the brothers had built without giving their penned stock something to nicker about.

Hereabouts the oaks were gnarled and stunted, mostly brush, mixed up considerably with thorny thickets of mesquite and catclaw. The drugged light of the moon, still furry and orange, didn't make things any better. Employing a great deal of care he skirted the barn, pausing a further while when the log walls of the house came blackly out of the piled-up shadows. There was still no sign of movement in the yard though he could see a huddle of stock behind the nearest rump to head in the small round corral that had the post in its center. He debated getting down off his horse but decided against this.

The place looked deserted. Grete didn't want to be caught with the appearance of sneaking up on his layout and if the brothers were gone he dared not risk any more time in scouting. With a prickly feeling between his squared shoulders he put the horse into motion, riding openly into the pale gloom of the yard.

Nothing happened until he got half across it when the geldings set up a racket from the horse trap, joined by the softer-pitched whickerings of the fillies. Grete reined up by the porch. "Hello, inside there—anybody home?"

He got out of the saddle and stepped up on the porch. He called again with his glance prowling the yard and this time heard the strained groaning of bunk ropes as someone turned over and slapped bare feet to the floor. Something sharply metallic, like a gun being cocked, came out of the sounds the man made moving around. It was the older brother's voice that called. "Who is it?"

"Trail boss—Farraday."

"Be right with you."

Grete heard the man pulling on his pants, then the slap of his weight crossing the boards of the floor. The door was yanked open. Something gleamed in the gloom. "What's up?" the man said.

"Where's your brother?"

"What difference would that make?"

There was. an edge of suspicion in the rancher's surly tone and this—coupled with the gun he had hold of—convinced Grete. He said, to throw the man off guard, "Take a look over here and tell me if this is him." He wheeled then, turning as though to cross the porch but coming all the way around. One down-chopping hand knocked the gun from the rancher's fist; Grete's other hand, lifting, cracked him wickedly across the throat. The man gagged, staggering back. Grete, coldly furious, smashed him in the face. The man went down as though hit with a club.

There was sweat on Grete's cheeks. With no waste of motion he stripped the belt from the man and lashed both wrists behind him. He caught up the man's shirt and worked the rancher's feet down into the sleeves, afterwards buttoning it all the way up. He stuffed the fellow's socks into his mouth and bound them in place with the rancher's dusty neckerchief. Satisfied then that he had done all he could, he quit the house, pulling the door shut after him, and got into the saddle.

At the gate of the corral where the fillies were penned he leaned down and yanked loose the top pair of rails. He took these with him off to the side, there letting go of them. "Hup, there—hup, hup!" he shouted, swinging his rope.

They went round the pen once showing

fright and bewilderment; then, ears laid back, they rose like hunters, sailing over the remaining rails as though this were something they did every day. A snap of Grete's rope sent them scampering up the trail. Not until he glimpsed the red eye of the fire through a cross-hatch of branches did Grete draw a full breath to curse the brother he had not found.

He didn't have to guess what the fellow was up to; he'd be scorching the sand getting word to Curly Bill. Even if the pair were truly bona fide ranchers they would feel this obligation—which was something he ought to have thought about sooner. Nobody ranched a country tucked away as this without some kind of a tie-up with wild ones.

A few more of these fool blunders and he'd be coyote bait! He was bone-weary, sure; but tiredness was no alibi. If a man couldn't keep his wits awake he'd no business getting mixed up with the kind of a crew Ben had hired for that girl. Grete swore again, bitterly.

He watched the fillies take off in the direction of the band and impatiently, testily, rubbed his aching eyes. The stars glittered coldly above dark jumbles of lava rock. The crew wasn't going to take kindly to any move order. Those riding herd would be looking to catch some sleep and. . .

Ben must have been watching for him. Grete was skirting the taller growth about the spring when Hollis came out of a shift of firelit shadows. "Wait—" he called.

Grete looked at him sharply, then got out of the saddle. He staggered a little, catching himself, aware of the peril of allowing it to become obvious how near he was to being out on his feet. He sloshed the reins at the man, too engrossed with the effort of trying to seem natural to notice that Hollis had been already reaching. "It's time to get moving."

"Couple of gents here," Ben said. "Maybe you better see them. I've an idea it might change some of your plans."

"What gents?" Grete stared blankly.

"Didn't mention their names—seemed to act like you'd know. They're over at the fire thawing out with some java."

Time was riding Grete hard and he was traveling in that half-land between sleep and waking or he'd have been more concerned. He swung away from the man. "Get those mares started out of here." He forced a way through the brush, each stride taking its toll of strength and energy. There was hardly any feeling in his legs, just solid weight. It was like boggy ground clutching his boots each time he moved them.

He pushed into the open, seeing the swirl of black shapes about the fire. He seemed to have a little trouble focusing, objects taking form as through a pitted glass. He managed to pick out Patch and the girl; he heard the grumble of cook's voice. Sombreroed Frijoles was off to one side, a little beyond Sary, firelight winking off the drilled peso of his chin strap; one of the new pair, with a tin cup in his hand, was facing this way. Grete had never seen either one of them before.

As he came nearer, the girl heard him and turned, mouth opening, but one of the strangers said quickly, "That's all right—I'll tell him." The fellow's hair was so blond it looked white in this light, like the hair of an albino; and the fire struck a flash from the front of his shirt as he moved to toss his emptied cup at cook's wreck pan. Only the cup wasn't empty.

Farraday saw the brief splash of spilled coffee, stupidly wondering why the man hadn't drunk it. He shoved a glance at the other man. Small cold eyes in a rock-hard face. A gash for a mouth and great hammy hands that, without regard for anything but trouble, were spread above the bulges of a pair of thonged-down leathers.

Farraday quit moving. "You boys looking for me?"

"If your name's Farraday, we are."

"Make it quick. We're pulling out."

The towhead grinned, showing teeth that had a lot of high-priced gold pounded into them. His sidekick said, "You're wanted in connection with the death of Irv French. You figure to come peaceable or tied belly-down?"

Grete turned completely still. He looked a long time at them, every tendon in his body stiffly, painfully alert. He scraped a hand across his cheeks. "You must have got hold of that by carrier pigeon. The guy ain't even stiff."

The towhead grinned. "We been trailin'—"

Farraday said contemptuously, "Where'd you leave your lanterns?"

"We've had enough gab," the bald-faced one said. "Turn loose of that belt."

Both men had badges. Though he had his own ideas about it, Grete didn't care where the badges had come from. He couldn't afford to let them take him and he was in no condition to put up a fight. He didn't reckon the crew would lift so much as a finger but he was wrong about that. While he stood there balancing his chances Ben said behind him: "You've lost your brass collar. Let go of it, buster."

Grete could tell by the pinched look of Sary's face Ben Hollis had a gun on him. The fellow wouldn't be needing much of an excuse to make it talk.

The thought left Grete with an irascible

frustrated sense of inevitability, a conviction this venture had been doomed from the start. "When a man beds down among wild animals I guess he oughtn't to complain if he collects a few teeth marks." He unbuckled the belt and felt the holstered weight of the Colt drop down his leg.

Ben said unctuously, "All right, gents, he's your coon. Take him."

NINE

Grete sighed bitterly as the two men, grinning, stepped away from the fire. "We'd have got him anyway," the towhead chuckled, "but your help won't be forgotten, fella. You might even come in for a piece of the reward."

"A man expects no reward for doing his bounden duty," Ben said loftily. "I've had my eye on this jasper ever since he tied onto this drive as trail boss. Just make sure he don't come back on us. We got trouble enough without—"

"He won't be back," Stone Face said, palming a pistol.

Grete didn't think so either as he stood woodenly watching their approach. These were Curly Bill men; everything about the pair lent credence to this conviction. They had smelled of the chaparral as far away as he could see them.

"Just a minute," Sary called. "I'm not guaranteeing one blessed thing but you two better stop right there."

"Sary—" Ben cried, sounding frantic, "keep out of this!"

She'd got the .44 out of her holster while the pair had been closing on Grete and now, having put their backs to her, both star-packers, frozen, were at a distinct disadvantage. It was like a problem in chess with every available piece irrevocably anchored.

If these truly were deputies they dared not turn their guns on a woman. And, far as that went, they dared not anyway for neither one of them, stopped flat-footed, was in any position to invite a general shoot-out. This crew was too scattered, too uncertain a quantity. The only thing, Grete knew, either stranger could be sure of was if guns started popping they'd be right in the thick of it.

Grete was in no better shape and his need was infinitely greater. They could pinch in their hands and sweat out another deal but Grete, if he could not extricate himself, was done for. He knew what he could expect once they got him away from the rest of this outfit. Yet he hung there, wound tight, unable to get off the horns of his dilemma.

He wanted, bad as ever in his life he'd wanted anything, to dive for the gun in that belt he'd let go of. But if he did, and Ben was ready, the man could cut him in two before his hand ever touched it.

The Mexican took the chance away from him. While Farraday stood rooted, Frijoles, stalking her like a cat, came behind the girl and, catching both arms within the circle of his own, jammed them tight against her hips, swinging her away from the strangers as he did so. Grete saw it all and couldn't open his mouth.

She could still have fired but nobody gave a damn; she no longer had it in her power to do anything more drastic than scuff up the landscape. Both strangers had jumped for Grete with their guns out the moment they realized her advantage was gone.

In an outburst of shame for the fears which had immobilized him Grete attempted, in exhaustions fettered fashion, to fight them off. A blow from Ben's gun barrel drove him to his knees. He was trapped in a nightmare of flashing fists and flying boots vaguely glimpsed through bursts of brilliant light, of blows that came out of nowhere until, battered insensible, he was no longer aware of anything.

The gabble of contentious voice sounds faded. The rhythmic shriek of leather warped protestingly against dry leather, the occasional tinkling of bit chains or the *ching* of a rowel stricking other equipment took its place in the half-world of hell Grete awoke to. Damp ground smells and horse sweat came up through the groan of his gun-hammered bones and his throbbing head felt big as a washtub; but this also passed. For a space everything was blackly silent and peaceful.

It was the jolt of the hip-shaken saddle grinding nauseously against the bruised muscles of his stomach that roused him finally to consciousness of his predicament and where-abouts in the peril of a threat achieved. He was traveling belly-down just as that rock-faced son had promised he would and the horse didn't care how much skin the brush took. The horse wouldn't care if Grete's head smashed into a rock!

He tried to work his navel off the hump but had no purchase from which to maneuver. The saddle was his anchor, it might soon be the last memory anyone would have of him—this picture of it toting him like a sack of grain to oblivion.

His head was splitting, throbbing almost unbelievably with every squeeze of his heart. There was a roar in his ears from all the blood pumped into them. The burn and bind at wrists and ankles convinced him that it would be his last ride. They didn't have to waste any lead on him. Just turn him loose on this pot-gutted cow, let out a few whoops at some appropriate interval, and geography and nature would combine to take care of him. Not nicely, perhaps, but permanently.

He twisted his head and found a brightness behind him, presently recognizing this for cook's fire receding through a forest of branches. When he discovered that, lying with his butt above his elbows, this gleam was below him, he knew the two strangers were heading for the pass.

He guessed the backs of his knees must be sprung beyond redemption. His feet were chunks of ice almost totally divorced from him, his hands filled with pins and needles. He tried doubling his fists to force some slack from the ropes; nothing gave except his patience. Whoever had tied these knots was an expert.

He guessed the voices he had heard must have come from the outfit, arguing. He drew little hope from this, since if they'd been of a mind to do anything they wouldn't have let Towhead and his two-gun friend load him onto this horse in the first place.

He might as well face it. He'd get no help from them. Ben was well satisfied to so easily have got shed of him; the Mexican, by his own act, was proved Ben's man. The drunken Rip cared for nothing but his everlasting bottle. Cook hadn't bothered to lift a finger.

There was the girl, of course, and Idaho. Sary wouldn't find a second chance—not with Ben back in place as Julius Caesar of this drive. Idaho was probably still with the horses.

He didn't know why he kept thinking of Idaho unless he could dredge up no other hope.

The gunfighter had little cause to care what happened to him; his face was still scarred with the marks of Grete's fists, his head ugly with scabs from the wreck of that bucket Grete had broken against it. He'd been prepared to tolerate Grete for the girl's sake, had made the exact extent of that tolerance plain. It had no conceivable bearing on Grete's present situation.

Grete dropped his glance to the skitter and blur on the ground passing under him. The footing was becoming noticeably rough. The breathing of the horses was a series of reaching grunts, the shod hoofs of the pair ahead rattling sharply against increasing contact with malpais, every sound growing larger. By these things Grete knew they'd entered the canyon and were climbing toward the pass. It was much darker here. Looking back he could no longer detect any sign of the camp. Not even the brightness which had marked cook's fire.

It was time for sober reflection, for last-minute adjustments of outmoded conceptions. Grete felt the walls closing in. Indescribably depressed, he listened to the wailing of a coyote on some close-by outcrop. He hardly realized for a moment that his horse had quit moving. Half strangled by hard-breathing excitement a voice said, "Let go of that rope an' sit tight in them saddles."

"Barney!" Grete choked.

After the badge-packers quit camp with Farraday roped belly-down to a horse confiscated from one of their work teams, Frijoles let go of the girl, jumping back with an alacrity which in other times might have dragged a smile from her. Now she hardly noticed. Sheathing the pistol he had kept her from using, she walked aross to where burly Ben was bent over a bed roll he'd just heaved down by the fire.

"You've got to go after him. Get Idaho and Rip. Take the whole crew if. . ." She stopped, eyes widening. Ben Hollis was laughing at her.

There was something at once smug and cruel in his face as he straightened and tipped back, sardonically regarding her. Standing there, teetering a little on his boot heels, he saw the satisfaction that had hold of him like new wine. A boldness, fire-bright, was possessively rounding the beads of his eyes as they ogled her breasts—almost, she thought, going furiously hot, as though they were bare with his hands wrapped around them.

Her skin crawled. How often had he fondled her like this without her knowing? She felt un-clean from the things that ran through his face and then, her own stiffening, she put away this ugliness and brought her will like iron staves about her feelings. "Patch!" she said. When no sound came she twisted to look at him, mouth squeezing into a bitter line.

Cook, stirring uncomfortably, pulled his shoulders together, staring back at her grumpily, not opening his mouth.

"Idaho will go," she said, and silence thick as fog came down. She saw Ben's grin and started for her horse. But the man was too quick, coming solidly in front of her. "He's bought and paid for—like the rest of this crew. Hereafter we're doing things my way, whether you like it or whether you don't."

She went up on her toes lashing out at him, cracking him across both cheeks with all her strength, the sound of the leathers loud as pistol shots. He caught her roughly against the great barrel of his chest, smothering her struggles,

90

tearing the quirt off her wrist and furiously breaking it. The stripes stood out like a brand across his face as he flung her away from him.

"You little slut!" he shouted, towering over her. He half-lifted a boot as though to bash in her ribs but some saner thought caught him and he stepped back, eyes ugly. "By God you'll crawl for that!" He was shaking all over with the wildness of his passion. "Get to your blankets!" he yelled, clenching his fists. He looked half-crazy in the flickering flames.

Cook scrubbed one hip with the flat of his hand, staring woodenly at her as she got up and stumbled off. Rip squirmed over in his bed and got his bottle. The Mexican's eyes flickered like black coals beneath his hat but Ben was not a man to cross right then. They kept their mouths shut.

Ben glared around a moment. "We pull out of here at daylight," he said, slamming into his saddle.

In her blankets Sary shivered uncontrollably. The cold got into her bones and ached and wherever her whirling thoughts tried to turn the man was there, towering over her, blocking every hole of escape she uncovered. If only, she thought, she could have hung onto Farraday . . . In the morning she would have to find a chance to talk with Idaho. He was her only hope now. She could not stand against Ben alone.

She heard him ride off, heard the cook and Frijoles mumbling under their breaths, then exhaustion claimed her. She was just falling into an uneasy doze when the dull clop-clop of hoofs came down through the trees to fetch the camp into wakefulness. She heard cook's smothered curse and the Mexican's *"Quien es?"* as, throwing back their blankets, they got half up, Frijoles drawing his sixshooter with his head jutting toward to peer into the dark.

She hadn't realized she'd been holding her breath until she heard Farraday's long, solid voice break through the muted cadence of hoof falls.

"Patch," he said, "rout out the crew."

TEN

Cook began banging on a pan with his pistol.

She watched the head of Grete's horse come out of the oaks. A second black shape coasted in behind Farraday, their elongated shadows tumbling over the ground as the animals came past the dying glow of the fire. She heard Barney's laugh, an irrepressible excitement quavering through his voice as he replied to some question the Mexican had asked. Now hoofs were coming at a lope from the holding ground. Patch dumped a load of dead branches on the fire and climbing flames flung a shower of sparks against the crushed-crystal glitter of faraway stars. Orange light drove back the solid dark and Ben's big shape appeared, followed by Idaho: Ben, catching sight of Grete, reined up so suddenly the gunfighter's horse stumbled heavily into him.

Grete said to Idaho, "Get those mares lined out for the pass right away."

No one moved. Idaho, curbing his fretful mount, turned his stare enigmatically on Hollis. Every eye in camp swung around to Ben now and this pressure, piling up, put the stain of outrage on the man's beefy cheeks. Even Farraday, though in the dark as to the why of it, understood the decision all were waiting for was

Ben's. Grete's own nerves, worn thin by the turmoil of these last several hours, boiled up a wicked impatience that sharpened the lines graved into his face and, pushed by the threat of Curly Bill's intentions which would be expedited now, he cried at Ben harshly, "Tuck tail or drag iron!"

The roundabout faces grew pinched and stiff and Ben's eyes hated all of them, shifting the blame for the bind he was caught in, absolving himself as he had done all his life. His face turned hungry with the lust to kill but his hand wouldn't move from its white hold on the saddle. He shook his head, cheeks poisonously bloated, eyeing first Idaho then, furiously, Grete. "What happened out there?"

It was Barney Olds' excitement-choked voice that, trembling with remembrance, said, "He killed that gunslick—cracked his skull with one of the fellow's own guns. But the towhead got away. We figure he's gone to fetch help."

"Curly Bill help," Grete said; and Ben's lips pushed out in a sullen pout. He peered at Grete, caught by indecision; but Sary, closely watching, found a shorter word for it. The man couldn't even find enough wind for bluster. He wrenched his fist from its clutch of the pommel and cut his horse through the blackness in the direction of the stock.

Idaho dragged his own horse around as the group broke up, Frijoles running for his mount. Cook, with his face warped to an even sourer cast, began cantankerously assembling supplies and culinary gear for packing. Idaho rode after Ben, the chin-strapped Mexican following. "Give Patch a hand, Olds," Farraday said, and went over to Sary where she stood at the edge of firelight. She lowered the pistol that was wet from her grip, thrusting it back of her, but not before Grete had glimpsed its metal gleam.

He stopped before her, discovering again how squarely defined her shoulders were, how straight her chin, how level her glance. He nodded toward the hand she held behind her, saying "Thanks," and continued to regard her with a long and thoughtful attention. It was in his mind to reveal the truth about that "ranch" she expected to share in, but he could not quite bring the words out. Instead he said, pretty gruff with his tone, "What do you hope to get out of this?"

She gave him back a look cool as his own. A little security . . . and peace." Always his face, when he looked at her, seemed to hold a kind of speculative reserve; it was a way he had of holding his lips as if he were not quite sure how to take her. These last hours had been hard on him; he looked like a saddle bum and a small edge of doubt crept into her thinking. Idaho' judgment ran through her head: *He'll use you as long as it suits his ends then find him some prettier, younger woman.* It kept her guard up. It made her distrust the lift of heart his nearness gave her.

Some knowledge, Farraday thought, steadily watching, hard-won and grim as death, had driven her in upon herself, forsaking the girl she might have been. Her hands, square-knuckled and strong, were used to work and, like the rest of her, capable beyond a woman's normal expectations. She was as near self-reliant as any girl he had met and, while he was not certain he favored so much character, he admitted that she would grow on a man. It was her silence, all the secrets behind it, which took hold of his interest—the mystery of her, he thought, detesting this. The still, strong acceptance of all she had been through, all she had seen; the indomitable will to survive which had brought her here with these stolen mares. These were the factors and her woman's body, combined with the tantalizing things he could guess at, which had built up the feelings he had about her.

"You think those two were Curly Bill men?"

"We'll find out."

His face seemed thinner, gaunt and sagging with fatigue. "Where," she asked, "did the one who got away go?"

"Through the pass."

"That's where we're going?"

"We haven't got much choice," he shrugged. "It's that or wait for Bill's main bunch." He loosed a shortbreathing laugh. "One of that pair at the ranch has lit out. They'll be coming up now from both sides of these hills."

He was a man ridden down to muscle and bone. She said without censure, "Some of the mares are pretty sore-footed."

"There's not much more of this. We'll be out of these rocks in a couple of hours if we can stay clear of trouble."

She could face facts. "You don't think we will." She watched his hands make an empty gesture.

"Somewhere," he said grimly, "we'll run into that bunch. Those badge-toters were scouts sent out to get a line on us. French simply provided a touch of luck they hadn't been looking for. When that towhead gets back they'll set up a trail block—probably send somebody off to find Bill. I want to hit them before Bill has time to come up."

Her eyes searched his face. "I think you

know by now how much dependence you can place on this crew."

"They'll fight. For their lives." He said, suddenly sharp, "Even a rat will do that!"

"Leaving Idaho out, that's what you're dealing with—rats. At the first whiff of trouble —real trouble—they'll run."

"Work stock's packed," Patch called from the shadows. "What about some mares for the rest of this stuff?"

"You'll have to let it go." Grete tipped his head, listening. "Mares are going into the pass now. You and Barney get started."

"They'll run," Sary repeated.

Farraday scowled. "Not this time they won't." He turned back for his horse, finding hers waiting beside it. Moon was pretty far down. Cook threw the rest of the coffee into the fire; dark closed around them while he anchored the pot to one of his saddle strings. They could see each other, that was about all. "Let's go," Grete said, and they swung into their saddles.

Near dawn they came into even rougher country. These past two hours had been anything but easy. The black lava rock was gone. This was a region of steep slants and gravel grown to greasewood. Occasionally cedars lifted gnarled branches against the paling stars. Riding the drag, along with Patch, the pack horses, and Barney Olds, Sary began to breathe easier in spite of the roughness of their travel; she began to hope Grete had been wrong about Bill.

Now and again they dipped into dry washes and plowed through deep sand until rocks or brush forced them out into sight with a clatter of scrambling hoofs as they climbed. Sometimes dust like a swirling fog closed the view, flour-thick and abrasive, until a downdraft of air from cooler heights returned blurred vision.

Farraday, up at the front now riding point, scanned the terrain closely in the brightening light, studying each lingering tatter of shadow hovering like smoke beneath paloverde and cat-claw, strengthening pitahaya columns and the low-lying studdings of mescal and Spanish bayonet. Behind such cover Bill's men could be, tawny wolves of the chaparral more deadly than Apaches.

There was no security in this land. It was a country of violence filled with wildness and terror, with deceptive sleepiness, the rip and blast of gunfire. Nothing was quite as it looked—nor so mild. It scoured the softness out of a man.

But the thought of her would not leave him. Beset as he was by the flight of time, harried by worries about Crotton and the ever-present dangers surrounding this drive, there was scant room in his itinerary for this kind of thing; yet she was clearer in his head than Swallowfork. He never had to turn to see her. Bright in memory was the way she had of holding herself, still and straight, when she looked at him, the light breaking across the sorrel surface of her hair. He remembered too well, he knew bitterly. This was what lay in the back of every man's head—the picture of some woman.

It was now gray day with the last of the shadow pockets breaking up, funneling away in misty stringers as morning advanced with the strides of a giant. The air turned colder with a sparkle of frost, sending the crew hunching into their windbreakers, this swift building up of light bringing out in sharpest focus every scarp and scallop of the ragged rims. Grete, standing up in his stirrups, peered around till his glance picked out Idaho. "Bring them on!" He swung a hurrying arm.

He pulled off to the side to let them pass, narrowing his eyes against the churned-up dust, irascibly swearing. Crotton by this time could have that meadow so commanded with guns the devil himself would be hard put to find toe-room. This was just one of the things gnawing Grete; another was the fellow who'd taken Grete's place with Crotton—a man whose memory might cause more trouble than all of Swallowfork's gunslingers. And Sary, Grete thought bitterly, had been right about these mares. Most of them already were showing sore-footed. They would have to lay over at Willcox. Someone would be sure to carry word to Crotton.

Bays, buckskins, sorrels, and roans, with a scattering of grays and blacks, stumbled past, pushed by the calls of the rope-swinging riders. They were traveling a natural trough through these hills, twisting and turning enough to break a snake's back. Now their dust would be flung up like a flag. He cursed that too.

Suddenly the sun was knifing into their backs, hurling its golden flood over everything, driving their shadows grotesquely ahead, miles long where they crossed a straight open. At once the chill faded. In an hour it was hot, with discarded jackets slung back of their cantles, sweat darkening the salt-rimed stains beneath armpits, lathering like soap on the flanks of the horses. Grete's weren't the only eyes watching the rimrocks.

The morning wore on. They nooned by a stream that was thick with willow and hack-berry, wolfing down the cold food passed around by Patch, more than one of them grousing the lack of hot coffee. It was on Grete's orders that no fire was kindled. He closed his eyes for a moment to ease the burn and, drugged by exhaustion, slept for two hours.

He awoke to find Sary's hand on his shoulder, stared at her stupidly, then sighted his shadow. He sprang up with a curse. Everyone else in camp was asleep. "God damn it," he snarled, "we got no time for foolishness—"

"You had to have rest."

"We could have woke up in hell!"

"I stayed awake. I've had more sleep than the rest of you." She saw the narrow-eyed way he was scowling into the west; he'd discovered the dust. "Wild horses," she said, and lifted a hand toward the stud. "Danny knows. We saw them crossing that saddle—"

The stallion's sudden trumpeting brought Idaho, bleary-eyed, out of the hackberries. The man hitched his gun up. The quick look he threw around cut the dust and swirled back. She saw the tightening about his jaw and mouth. Farraday nodded. "Get those fools on their feet."

"It's only horses," Sary said. "The stud—"

"Horses sure," Idaho grumbled.

"And something pushing them," Farraday said. His tone was dry as snapping sticks. The girl stared uneasily from one to the other. "I saw them crossing that saddle—"

"You can't see them now. Wild stock don't travel like that without they're pushed. Those horses are running."

Idaho's shout brought the men off the ground. "Put those mares in the creek—"

"Too late for that. They know we're here." Grete frowned at the canyon walls. "We can't climb out this side of that saddle; if we get that

100

far there won't be no point to it. Bowie's not over five miles right now. Bunch the stock. We'll make a run for it."

ELEVEN

Here where they'd nooned, the walls of the canyon, perhaps a hundred yards apart, ran straight for an approximate quarter of a mile. At this point, dropping, they swung north in a series of twisting convolutions, then went angling south in a kind of battered crescent as they converged on the saddle, or low notch, the girl had mentioned. There, in Grete's recollection, they fell away entirely to form the table-flat bench which could be seen from here. The abrasive haze his eyes were focused on hung directly over the very gut of the passage where the pinched-in walls stood scarcely twenty feet apart. Grete, reviewing these facts, sat motionless. The crew was mounted, the mares were bunched, a sullen quiet came out of the way these scowling men sat waiting for orders.

Still Farraday watched the yellow creep of that dust drift nearer. It was barely a mile away, say a mile and a half if you were counting the bends. Bill's understrappers, if Grete had the right of this, were using those broncs to mask their approach. Gauging pace by the dust, he decided they'd be burning powder within the next hour. Very possibly sooner.

Like a general Grete's look went over the ground. A poor spot for defense and, without memory lied, nothing better to be found this side of the gut. Little cover, no shelter, no good chance for an ambush. But they didn't have to sit and wait for Bill's wolves. . .

"Come on," he said, throwing up an arm; but Ben kicked his grulla out in front of Grete, stopping him. "Man, you sure ain't figurin' to go meet that bunch—"

"Why not?"

The girl's chunky brother-in-law looked at him aghast. "God's galluses, Farraday! If that's Curly Bill's bunch you might's well shoot us down like dogs!"

"You got a better suggestion?"

"I say, by God, let's get outa here—"

"Afoot? You can't take a horse out of this canyon short of that saddle—"

"We can go back the way we come—"

"Go ahead if you've got the stomach for it. One of that pair at the ranch pulled out last night. If he's done what I figure, you'll find yourself faced with some more of Bill's wolves. Way I see it they're closing in from both ends." Grete's look swept the rest of them. "You can die like a rat in their trap or you can fight. I'm electing to fight," he said, and picked up his reins.

There was a kind of bleak quiet while all hands stared at Idaho. You couldn't tell what went on behind those raw-red cheeks still scuffed and scabbed with the marks of Grete's fists and the bucket Grete had broken against the man's bony head. The gunfighter's shrewd, part-closed eyes touched Sary, then moved unreadably at Grete. "You're the boss. Give your orders."

Grete didn't know if he was relieved or more worried, but this was no time to be unraveling riddles. "They know we're in front of them but maybe not how far. We're in no position to try

103

any traps but we can, if we go at this right, throw those damn broncs right back in their laps. With this drive coming down on them hellity-larrup they're going to have to drag cotton and dig for the tules. Short of that saddle, they'll have no chance to pull up and make a fight of it—not if we hit them right. If we push these mares hard enough we ought to be onto them before they can get set."

Idaho, studying that, finally nodded. "They won't see our dust. But it's like to be hell with the clapper off when this drive smashes into them wild ones."

"We're going to have to chance that. We'll lose stock, but if we bring them up slow Bill's boys will empty some saddles. There'll be enough powder burnt when we come onto that bench. Shoot all you want, keep the mares bunched if you can, but once you're in the open don't stop," he said grimly, "or you won't ever leave there."

He slanched a last look around, raised an arm, and the crew, shaking ropes out, got the mares on the go. Dust boiled up in a pounding of hoof sound. The mares broke into a run, gathering speed. They rocked into the first twirl of the wriggles and twists. They were slowed by the turns, whooped ahead by the yelling. Right and left they weaved, scraping rock, crowding, jostling, shrilly squealing, swapping leads in perfect unison and, heckled by the shouts and ropes, filling the passage like a wall of water.

Sweat dripped off the men, darkened and lathered the coats of the horses. Racket came off the walls like bedlam, echo piling on echo until the stock went crazy with it. The eyes of the mares wildly rolled in their sockets as they broke out of the twists and poured into the narrowing hoop of the crescent.

Neither side knew where the other was now. They met head-on in full career, shock reaching back into the drag of both outfits. Screams and terror jammed the passage. The batter of sound was constant. Dust boiled up until the way was choked with it. Thick as a pea-soup fog it billowed, strangling, blinding, wave on wave, pulsating, oscillating, eddying and whirling until a man could hardly find the horse between his legs.

But the drive, Grete realized, had never quite stopped. It had staggered and slowed, but the weight of momentum, of close-packed numbers, was pushing it irresistibly on through the dust and the high thin screams of mangled flesh. Now the crew was firing over the heads of the drag, stampeding the pack animals into the crush. The pace picked up—Grete could see the packs jouncing. The whole drive began to run. Sun came through in shining tatters and lances until presently, vaguely, like something glimpsed through sanded glass, Grete could see the far shapes of frantic horsemen quirting.

The crew saw them, too, at once unlimbering their rifles. This firing and yelling, the steady pressure of sound driven back and forth and redoubled by echo, drove the mares into headlong flight. Up front Curly Bill's desperate men were flogging their mounts in a panic. Grete saw two go down, one horse briefly rising like a stick thrown out of a log jam. A yell sheared thinly through the uproar and was gone.

Now he saw the bench opening out in front of them, saw the outlaws madly spurring to quit the bench at either side. One fellow, arms and legs pitched out grotesquely, bounced off his horse backwards, mouth stretched wide in an unheard yell. Another man, with a blue coat flapping round him, clutched his chest, all control of his mount abandoned. Bill's men were too busy trying to save themselves from being run down to have any time or thought for their weapons. Grete saw Ike Clanton's chalk-white face and the whiskered mat of Jim Hughes' cheeks behind a fist-shaken carbine. Then they were past, rifles popping back of them, the mares stringing out in a dash across the open, the crew spurring up on either flank, trying to close them up into threes or fours so that when they reached the bench's far end they could funnel them into the black slot of the canyon. Grete could see the gash with its red-yellow walls where the trail found passage through these tumbled hills.

Up ahead of him a pack horse went down as though axed, spilling its load and flipping all the way over, one frantic hoof catching the rump of Grete's horse, almost knocking him into Sary's gray which shied violently, nearly unseating her. Ben's horse was hit and losing ground steadily; Grete saw the Mexican drop back, kicking a foot from the stirrup, and then something pulled his glance again to Sary. The gray was stumbling; there was blood on its hip. Farraday kneed his horse closer. Now they were neck and neck. The gray's eyes were wild. Grete threw an arm out, shouting at the girl, but she shook her head at him, keeping the horse on its feet with the reins. Grete, swearing, furious, crowded his own mount against them. "Kick your feet free!"

Not even her strength on the reins was going to keep that gray going many more strides. Its head was coming down; Grete knew it was running blind. "Kick loose!" he shouted, and caught the girl about the waist.

He wasn't a moment too soon. As her knee

cleared the cantle the gray's legs went out from under it. Grete's look, darting ahead of them, found the mares pouring into the slot. He had never seen a more welcome sight than those canyon walls as they opened in front of him.

He let the girl slide down as soon as they got into the dropped rocks from the cliff. Yanking his rifle, he got out of the saddle and, tossing her the reins, ran back through the dust to have a look at what was happening.

"Reckon they've had a bellyful," Idaho said, coming beside him.

Only three of the outlaws were still in sight. Jim Hughes, Ike Clanton and the badge-packing towhead. They sat their jaded horses back where the drive had first come onto the bench and there was nothing about their appearance to indicate an intention of carrying this further.

"Nevertheless," Grete said, "we'll be keeping our eyes peeled. There's still barren country between us and Willcox."

TWELVE

Against Ben's grumbling and Sary's vigorous
protests they by-passed Bowie, giving it plenty
of elbow-room. Grete was taking no needless
chances of being further delayed this side of
safety. He was on his dun with a rope around its
jaws in lieu of the bridle he'd loaned the girl
along with his saddle; Ben was forking Frijoles'
hull. With a rifle in his arms Grete ranged far
and wide, keeping constant watch. But they saw
no more of the marauders. Either Bill hadn't
come up with his main bunch or had decided any
additional attempt against the drive was no
longer feasible. If the latter were the case, Grete
thought their present whereabouts might have
considerable to do with it. For they were in
country now where in the past Bill had preferred
to exhibit his good behavior.

The drive pulled into Willcox on the
following night and a more whipped-out bunch
of hooligans a fellow never looked at. Dust-
streaked and brush-scarred, unshaven, bleary-
eyed, and generally acting like hell wouldn't
have them, they set up a camp out from the east
edge of town where broad grassy flats made
keeping track of the stock relatively simple.

"First thing I want," Sary said, "is a bath."

Grete could understand that; the same
thought was in his own head. He stood a

108

moment rasping grimy beard-stubbled cheeks, hard eyes picking over the rest of the outfit. "We've got to rest up these mares. I'll take you in. You can put up at the hotel."

She gave him and unreadable look. "I can find it."

"You're not about to go in by yourself."

"I'll take her in," Ben said, reaching his coat down. "I've—"

"You're staying here. And that goes for the rest of you." Grete looked around. He got some pretty hard stares. No one talked back but he could read reservations in the cant of their jaws. "Our friend Bill ain't the only thief in this country. This stock's going to be watched. You'll do no hobnobbing with strangers."

"A man's spare time," cook said, scowling, "is his own."

"When you've got some spare time I'll see that you know about it."

There was no further talk. Grete took Sary into town and saw that she got a decent room at the hotel. The clerk was inclined to be garrulous but a second look at Grete made him hobble his tongue. Outside her door Grete said, "I'll leave your horse at the livery. If you want it, send for it; don't go out on the street by yourself without you're mounted."

He saw her chin lift. "I'm used to taking care of myself—"

"Mind what I'm telling you," he said curtly, and left her.

On the street he debated dropping in on the marshal but decided against it. Folks would know he was back soon enough without him helping it. He got into the saddle and walked his horse back to camp.

The mares he thought, looking them over, seemed quiet enough. He swung down by the fire, more used up than he knew, wishing now he'd stopped off at a barber's. A hot soak in a tub would have taken some of this out of him.

He hauled the gear off his horse and turned it loose with a slap, stood listening a while to the snores of the crew. He moved around, counting shapes. All here but one.

Remotely angry, he looked again. One of the shapes, twisting over, came onto an elbow. It was the kid. "I left your roll over there with Patch's stuff."

"Where's Rip?"

Olds replied too quick. "Said somethin' about keeping an eye on the stock."

Farraday could guess what kind of stock that was. He thought, *To hell with it!* He went over and opened his bed, kicked off his boots and got into it; as an afterthought he pulled off his hat. He lay there a moment more dead than alive. Swearing under his breath he reached down and unbuckled his gun belt and, arching his back, dragged its lumpiness from under him. His wind came out in a long sort of sigh. Still he didn't feel right. He pushed an arm out and brought the hat over his face and went to sleep with a fist curled around the bone grips of his pistol.

In spite of the log-like quality of his slumber he awoke at the first sound of stirring. He sat up in his blankets to find day at hand, the black crags of the Peloncillos brightly edged with silver where they touched the horizon. Cook was hawking and spitting like a man well into the last lap of consumption. The kid, Barney Olds, was breaking dead wood Patch had salvaged from their trek through the canyon, and the gunfighter, with a handbuilt limply plastered to his lip, was staring unreadably through the curl of its smoke from a perch on the folded-up bulk of his tarp.

Olds got a fire going while cook stirred up batter.

Frijoles in the middle of a snore suddenly sneezed and presently, flinging back his blankets, stomped into his boots and lit out for some buckbrush, the only thicket in sight. Farraday glanced toward the horses, discovering Rip riding circle.

The sun hooked its chin above the peaks and poured a burst of pure light across the valley's empty acres, gilding the distant roofs of town, striking bright dazzles from east-facing windows. Beyond the gunfighter Hollis threw covers off his head. He scrubbed his eyes and blinked around and swore and crawled out and got into his pants. He scowled when his stare piled up against Grete. "We're out four mares and a nag from the work teams." By his tone he made it seem these facts were entirely Farraday's fault.

Grete ignored him but the kid, straightening up, was plainly minded to speak out. He had his mouth half-open but after a quick look around he caught up a rope and went off toward the horses.

Coffee smell began to lace through the camp. Over the fire salt pork commenced to crackle and Patch, hunching over it, began cutting up spuds into half a Dutch oven. Idaho, grinding out his smoke, looked up as Grete pulled on his boots. "You got somethin' in mind for this mornin'?"

Observing the way the man brightly watched from behind half-shut lids—listening more to the voice than to what it was saying—Farraday came fully around, tugged and swayed by his own quicker breathing. A

111

wildness drifted across the feel of these things and Idaho pushed a thin grin over his teeth, all the cocked joints of his body crouched and tightened. Yet, in some obscure way, he seemed not entirely ready—not, at least, quite willing to bring the gun up into his hand.

It wasn't fear. There was no fear in him. And no forgiveness.

Farraday's glance cut over those others. "Cook's going into town to stock up. He'll be glad to fetch back anything you boys want." He said after a moment, "Barring whisky and women," and let the stillness pile up for a laugh that never came. "Both today and tomorrow we're going to be right here." Some of their ill temper got into his own face. "It might be that last night I didn't make myself plain. Nobody leaves this camp without my permission."

Rip rode up and dropped out of the saddle. The kid came in with Grete's dun and two others caught up from the carry. Patch said, "Come an' git it."

They filled their plates in a sullen quiet, squatting where the notion stuck them, each with his cup of steaming java. There was no talk, no feeling of comradeship a man could look back on, nothing holding them together but avarice and hate. There was no real difference between these men and that bunch they'd come through back there in the hills. They were cut from the same cloth, moved by similar appetites. Ordinary give and take, common decencies, didn't touch them. They were held together by their greed for Sary's horses, and all that stood in the way of this was their fear of Grete and Idaho.

Grete saw this clearly. The silence was thick with it. And he saw with a pitiless clarity how alike he and the gunfighter actually were. It was not a palatable comparison or one he was able any longer to avoid. *Gunslick!*

He might hide from the aptness of the term in his own mind but deep down inside he understood King Crotton as he never had before. This was how Crotton must have seen him; here, stripped of pretense, had been the basis of their relationship. Never the friend he had imagined himself to be. Just another hired gun. Treated well, to be sure—like a fine suit of clothes or a horse hard to come by. He understood now why Stroat, methodical, unimaginative, had been passed over for himself.

Stroat had the job now—the man would be a real broom with it.

Grete bolted the last tasteless mouthful of food, choking it down, getting up just as Rip did. Rip's eyes slid around, springing wide as Grete stepped up to him. Grete's hard glance found the sag in Rip's coat; his hand, stabbing out, came away with the bottle. "Lock this up," he said, tossing it to Patch.

Cook, lips locked tight, kept his hands where they were, flinching aside just enough to avoid being hit. Rip's bottle, striking the Dutch oven, shattered. Rip's bugged-out eyes watched the precious liquid run across the sooty metal and become an inch of darkness in the dust of the trampled ground. The sound he made was like the scream of a hamstrung pony. He got a knife from somewhere and with the face of a wild man sprang for Grete.

Rage gave him twice the strength his frame warranted. That first swing almost skewered Grete. Too late he realized he could not watch all of them, that here was what they had likely been waiting for—a chance to gang up on him. It was in their faces, in those widesprung eyes, in the cat-quick way they all came onto their feet. He

113

had to watch Rip. The man was rushing in again, face twisted, the shine of his eyes throwing out a turned-loose fury that had no light of reason in it.

A dozen futile thoughts whirled through Grete's head. The glint of that blade was wicked as a snake's tongue. There was gooseflesh at the back of Grete's neck and a cold sick horror at the pit of his belly. Naked steel had this power.

He knew Rip meant to gut him.

He could go for his gun—the impulse was in him, but if he set hand to pistol other guns would lift. It was not fright of a shoot-out which stopped him but the certain knowledge of what a corpse-and-cartridge occasion would do to the plans he hugged for besting Crotton. Every man of this crew would be needed at Swallowfork.

Ducking, stumbling, forced around in a circle by the darting lunges of that glittering steel, Grete no longer knew where any of them were except the kid, Barney Olds, whom he could glimpse now and again against the blur of light and shadow that made a backdrop for the savage slashes of Rip's blade. The rest, he guessed, must be someplace back of him. His only defense was constant motion, to be continually moving until he could manage to get inside Rip's reach.

Olds appeared again behind Rip, plainer now, evidently nearer, his white cheeks stiff with tension. The boy, nerved up to something, was working closer. Now Rip, stertorously breathing, abruptly shifted and commenced to back off. The kid suddenly stuck a leg out, intending to trip Rip. But Rip, again making one of those lightning shifts, lunged forward as though to pass Grete, spinning in mid-career to drive straight in, forcing Grete around. Grete, jumping frantically back, tripped over a loose rock and went down, heavily jarred, all the breath spilling out of him. Stretched like that he scarcely heard Idaho's shouted "Stand fast!" that stopped all the rest of them dead in their tracks. Grete was conscious in that moment of nothing but Rip's eyes and the glass-bright shimmer of the knife in Rip's fist.

THIRTEEN

Refreshed by her bath and a night between sheets Sary, awake much too early, permitted herself the luxury of dawdling abed until the sun, coming through the window's cracked blind, shamed such an extravagant waste of good daylight. Stretching, deliciously yawning, she presently sat up and shook out her red hair, suddenly enticed by the prospect of eating in town. There'd be eggs and ham—all manner of "throat-ticklin' grub" as Patch would scornfully have put it; and perhaps, she thought with a confusion of feelings, there would be Grete Farraday.

Still thinking about him she threw back the covers, slid her legs out from under and, pushing up, crossed the uncarpeted floor to the washstand. The mirror disclosed little she had not observed before.

She frowned, shaking her head, at what sun and dust, branch water and wind were doing to her complexion. But she gave this only a passing thought, having long ago discovered she hadn't a face men would turn about to stare at—attractive enough—she had good eyes—but a vast way from being any step to sudden riches. She had integrity and courage, a certain amount of ingenuity; but what man, she wondered with a touch of dry humor, ever bothered to look at a woman's character!

She poured alkaline water into the chipped basin, wet a corner of the dingy towel, and washed the sleep from her eyes. She combed out her hair and put it up, still thinking of Farraday. Turning away from the glass she got into her clothes and took the chair off the knob and stood a moment, suddenly sighing. Opening the door she took a last look around and went down the stairs.

He wasn't in the lobby. No sign of him in the dining room. She held her disappointment under careful restraint, not at all sure of her feelings. She was giving too much thought to the man. She remembered his face, the sharp gray of his eyes, the tough way he had of sizing things up. He was opinionated, heavy-handed, entirely too... Well, too what? she asked irritably. Too ready to take his way by force? Wasn't this why she had wanted him?

She found a table in a corner, ordering in-differently, engrossed in the enigma of human relationships. When the food came she ate it, the pleasure foreseen in the prospect unrealized. Two drummers across the room sat with papers folded at elbows, heads together, chuckling, the one with his back to her occasionally turning to reveal an appraising, speculative glance. She ignored them.

A man with handlebar mustaches and a star on his vest drifted in from outside, looked around and pulled a chair out, roughly halfway between Sary's place and the drummers. She watched the waitress bring coffee. The man laid both elbows on the table and left the black hat on his head. "Any rain east of the mountains?"

"Dry as a bone," answered one of the drummers.

The marshal wasn't drinking his coffee, Sary noticed. Just sitting there, vacantly staring into space. She finished her breakfast, looked at the bill, and laid a half dollar on the cloth beside it.

The lawman came out of his chair before she did. A sudden coldness crept into her when she saw him cut around a near table, coming toward her.

He came up with an easy, half-smiling glance. He took the hat off his head and laid a hand on the table. She noticed the blunt square shape of his fingers. "You with them horses camped east of town?"

Sary made herself nod. "We're taking them out to the ranch," she said.

"And may I ask where that is, ma'am?"

"Why—" She stopped with her mouth open, belatedly realizing she didn't know where it was, didn't know even what name it was called by. "Grete Farraday's ranch."

He just stood there, not speaking. He said, "I see," rather strangely, she thought, as though he didn't see at all. "Grete Farraday," he nodded, and appeared to be studying something over her head. "You know Grete pretty well?"

"I'm his partner."

She didn't like the still, unsmiling manner of his regard or the odd offbeat way those blunt fingers tapped the table. She said, "Is he in trouble?"

"Oh no—no," he said—"no trouble that I know of. Whereabouts did you fetch this stock of horses from ma'am?"

"We brought them through from New Mexico."

"Through Stein's?"

Something about the way he was watching her suggested to Sary she might be on dangerous ground. She said frankly, "No. Grete brought us through some pass to the north of Stein's."

He seemed to be turning that over. "Well," he said, "let's ride out there," and put on his hat, taking the hand off her table.

Sary rose, slipping into her jacket. There was something here that she wasn't quite getting. She searched his face. "Is there a quarantine—something I might not know about?"

"No. Nothing like that. You'd have been stopped anyway if you had come through Stein's. Brands'll have to be looked at. Just a routine check," he said, smiling.

She followed him out, not at all reassured. On the street she said, "I've got a horse at the livery. . ."

"I'll go with you," he said, and swung into the saddle.

Flat on his back with all the breath jarred out of him, Grete Farraday watched the man gather himself. For what seemed an eternity he lay in a kind of drugged stupor. It was the fright in the kid's voice suddenly crying "Boss— boss!" that jerked Grete out of his paralysis. Desperately he twisted, digging his boots in, knowing he hadn't any time to get his legs up.

Rip's weight plummeted into him, smashing him back, but the blade instead of skewering him passed through the slack of his shirt, going into the ground like a picket pin, holding him so that he was not at once able to twist himself free. He pounded Rip's head, battered his kidneys. The man got a forearm wedged across Grete's throat.

Farraday forced a knee up, arching his back. Rip's weight slid a little but he had one leg still flung across Grete, trying off-balance to get enough purchase to wrench his knife out of the ground. Grete sought that wrist, clamping down on it, at the same time succeeding in getting his other knee up. Rip's weight slid some more.

Only the upper portion of him now held Grete down. Grete, half-strangled from the pressure of Rip's arm, tried again to dislodge him and, failing, flung up both legs and got one wedged between them. Sweat-drenched, gasping, he pushed outward and downward, tearing Rip away from him, tipping the man over, breaking Rip's grip on the knife.

Grete tore loose of it and rolled, coming onto his feet just as Rip scrambled up. They were both breathing raggedly. Rip, still running on rage, slammed into him, striking, snarling, striking again. Those were punishing blows and Grete, giving ground, felt every one of them.

He shook his head, trying to find the man. Something out of nowhere cracked him hard across the nose, numbing the whole inside of his face. Then he saw Rip and smashed him on both sides of the neck. The man swayed groggily. Grete drove a knee full into Rip's belly.

The man's chin came down like a black-smith's apron. As he stumbled forward Grete hit him twice more. The man reeled away with his mouth sprung wide, going wabble-kneed round in a kind of half-circle. He grabbed his face in both hands, collapsing into the dust.

The violence of the fight was still a wicked-ness in Grete's stare. His head felt about to burst loose from his shoulders. Before he could speak, Barney Olds, coming around Frijoles, caught a glimpse of Ben Hollis queerly peering toward town. The kid, following that glance, discovered an approaching pair of horsebackers. He stared hard at these two. He said, "Company comin'."

Something uneasy in the sound of it pulled Grete's head around. He recognized both of them. Sary and Ed Stamper. Stamper was marshal of Willcox, a hard man to fool and an honest one. Grete wished now he had stopped in to see the man.

He walked over to the water bucket and sluiced his face. He cuffed some of the dust off his clothes, stuffed in his shirt, and poured the rest of the water over Rip.

The man groaned and spluttered. Grete nudged him with the toe of a boot. "Onto your feet—"

"What the hell did you hit me with?"

"Next time," Grete said, "it'll be an ax handle. Pick up that bucket and go fill it with water." He sent a sharp look at Hollis, but Ben like the rest of them was eyeing the newcomers. Their hoof sound quit in a chorus of whinnyings. Grete swung around.

"So you've come back," Stamper said. "With a crew and a partner."

"You come all the way out here just to tell me that?"

"I had to see it to believe it." The marshal's stare washed over the rest of them, considering the girl, going back to Grete's face. "I gave you credit for better judgment."

A dark unruliness came into Grete's look. The marshal still eyeing him, let the silence build up. Grete said coldly, "I know what I'm doing."

Stamper nodded. "Do these others?"

"It's not your concern."

121

Ben's head came around. Idaho's eyes took on a deeper and darker searching. The Mexican, Frijoles, cocked his soft-shining eyes inquiringly at Ben. The kid looked nervous.

Sary's voice bridged the uneasy quiet. "Mr. Farraday has my completest confidence. Whatever he believes we should do will be done."

"Why, ma'am," the marshal said, "I am sure of that."

Grete smiled with his teeth but did not invite Stamper to get out of the saddle. The lawman, glancing around, said as though he were discussing the weather, "Whereabouts do these horses hail from?"

Farraday stiffly watched the man. "Aren't you kind of stepping out of your bailiwick, Marshal?"

"Matter of opinion."

They considered each other, Farraday's eyes angrily brightening. "A marshal's right to ask questions does not extend beyond the limits of the town that pays his wages."

Stamper smiled. "Want to look at my credentials?"

Farraday, sensing a trap, shook his head. "I just don't like to see a woman pushed around."

"You know me better than that, Grete."

Farraday, trying to keep one eye on the crew, said, "This stock came out of Texas—" and was at once aware without glancing at the girl that she had given a different answer. It was in the thin grin that crept about Stamper's eyes, in the way he quietly sat there, left hand idly playing with the reins.

A pale rage sparkled in Grete's stare.

Stamper said, "I'll take a look at them," and was turning his mount when something about Grete's stance pulled his face around. "Don't be a fool!" he cried sharply.

Farraday's eyes were black as lamp soot. He had the look of a prodded tiger. He snatched up a halter shank off the ground and, stepping over to the horses Olds had fetched, wrassled it around the jaw of one. Ignoring the animal's flattened ears he heaved himself up, curbing its action with the rope. He saw Rip slogging back with the bucket. Olds came up and handed him the pistol he hadn't missed. Grete took a look at its barrel and shoved it into his holster and, bringing up his black stare, sent the horse after Stamper.

All this while Ben had kept his mouth shut. Now he said to Olds, "Put my rig on that black."

Sary looked from him to Idaho, understanding with her woman's intuition that each of these after his fashion coveted her. "Is this wise?"

The gunfighter's raw-red cheeks stayed unreadable. Olds, still unmoving, had his eyes fixed on Sary. Anger whipped into Ben's handsome face. "Did you hear me!" he yelled.

Farraday, coming up to the stock with the marshal, growled, "What are you up to?"

Stamper's face swung about. "That's one thing I don't have to ask you."

"Never mind! This stock is no concern of yours—"

"You better listen to me, Grete," Stamper said to him. "The complexion of things around here is changing. I'm a deputy brand inspector now and there's another at Stein's as you would know if you'd come through there. I want to know why you didn't."

Grete said more reasonably. "I had word Curly Bill might be looking for us there."

"Who tipped you off?"

"Matter of fact it was French."

"French!" Stamper peered at him oddly.

Farraday grinned. "He sure as hell didn't aim to. Somebody had fed Miz' Hollis a yarn that folks over here was purely crying for good horse stock. Somewhere French had latched onto her, claiming he would find her a buyer for the lot. He showed up the day after I had made my deal and allowed he had buyers lined up at Stein's."

"So you pointed 'em north. Where'd Bill's bunch hit you?"

"Came down on us in that canyon east of Bowie. Ike Clanton, Hughes, and some more of that stripe."

Stamper stared at the horses, slowly circling the band. "Flyin' H," he said, pulling up to look closer. "That stud's got class. Better mannered than most." And then he said, "Texas brand. . . . The girl said New Mexico. You got any ideas about that?"

"She came out of that country—that's where I ran into her. Probably didn't rightly catch your meaning."

The marshal, without comment, reached into his saddlebags. He fetched out a brand book and thumbed through its pages. "Here we are—Flyin' H. Tate Hollis. Brady, Texas—that the one?"

"Tate was her husband's name."

"Was? Is he dead?"

"That's what I understand."

"What'd he die of?"

"By God, Stamper! Why don't you ask her!"

"I probably will," Stamper said, putting the book back. "Now I'll tell you something, Farraday. Swallowfork ain't got one friend in this country and, as Crotton's ramrod these past four years, I guess you know about how popular you are." He held up a hand. "All right, that don't bother you. It don't bother me, either, but when you flimflam a woman into—"

"Stamper," Grete snarled, jerking his chin up, "don't say it!"

"I'll say it. I want this out in the open. I don't want you claimin' after it's too late you didn't catch my meanin'."

Watching Farraday, the marshal saw the unbridled leap of rage throwing its glare up into the desperate, affronted look of him, burning away the tie-ropes of his temper. All the wild and reckless pride of the man's unbending nature was in the white flash of those suddenly bared teeth—all the aroused intolerance of an established way brought headlong up against the granite face of change. He was, Stamper thought, as adamant as Crotton. He had been raised in Crotton's shadow, time and again bitterly shown that might made right; this doctrine had been nourished with every chapter of his experience. He had become too conversant with its grim rules to relish change; he meant to carve a place for himself by following Crotton's footsteps.

All of this Ed Stamper had previously suspected, sure of it when Farraday had filed on that best piece of Crotton's vast unpatented range. He had seen it coming and now it was here. Farraday had learned Crotton's lessons well. Swallowfork had sown the crop of fury about to be reaped and if Crotton was to die of it he would be getting no more than his just deserts; but, damnably, innocent men must die, for it was ever that way in a contest of strength. Others would be sucked into this feud, men on the fringes, other ranchers and squatters over whom King Crotton had ridden roughshod on his climb to empire, masterless men whose guns were for hire, the army of saddle tramps who had nothing to take into this fight but hate and who would seize this chance of coming out heeled. The marshal, a Texan, had seen feuds before. The entire region would suffer while a handful of men, made bold by their plunder, were fattening on misery; and who would remember those who fell by the way?

"Be hell on the women an' livestock," he said. With his tone going rougher he mentioned the rest of it, the broken homes and the heartbreak, the men with families who would be pulled into it, those with old grudges, the dispossessed—"but I expect you're countin' on them."

Grete stayed silent, his face stony set, his look hard as agate. Stamper sighed. "Well, so be it." He pulled his horse around and then swung back with his own gusty temper. "Just remember this, Farraday, when the widows an' kids is plantin' the dead ones. Their blood will be on your hands. You won't ever get it off."

He saw that he was wasting his breath but he said: "There's one other thing, this woman you've tied into this—what does she stand to get out of it? You're usin' her crew and her horses. What'll she—"

He broke off, skreaking around in the saddle to see Ben spurring up on the black, the girl following. Ben skidded the horse to a stop on its haunches. "That fellow," he cried, flinging a hand square at Grete, "killed a man and I saw it—shot him down like a dog!"

Stamper's eyes fastened on Grete, moved narrowly back at his accuser. "What man?"

Ben's stare brightened with malice. "I

126

think they called him French—"

"He was a dog," Stamper said, and departed.

FOURTEEN

They pulled out in the night and made a number of miles before going into camp under a grove of live oak where the dark was so thick a man could pretty near cut it. "No fire," Grete said, "and no smoking till sunup. Two men on guard. If you see anything moving, knock it down."

The kid said thinly, "Is this Injun country?"

"Still a few bucks prowling through these hills."

But it wasn't Apaches Grete had on his mind. This was Swallowfork, and Crotton's crew wasn't likely to waste many words with outsiders.

Farraday had been hard to get along with ever since the marshal's visit and even after he'd rolled into his blankets his black thoughts stayed bitterly with him. Ben had been walking pretty soft since his rebuff from Ed Stamper, but he was one who had to be watched and that cross-grained wooden-legged cook was another.

While the marshal was with him Patch had gone into town after the supplies Grete had sanctioned and an hour and ten minutes later, riding in to see what was keeping him, Farraday discovered cook hadn't been to the store. He'd spent another twenty minutes picking up the deserter's trail and the rest of that day catching up with the fellow and fetching him back. Grete knew the man would put a knife in him if he ever got the chance. And there was Rip and his broken bottle and Frijoles who looked to Ben for instruction. And any time now he might be up against Idaho. A hell of a prospect to go into a fight with.

They were up at first daylight, wolfing down Patch's chuck. Salt pork and whistleberries downed with java so black it left a stain on the cups. They were moving by six, and by eight half the mares were sore-footed and limping. Nothing to be done but cut the pace down to a snail's crawl.

Tempers turned ugly and at ten, in higher country, going into a loop to approach Texas Canyon, Sary dropped back to where Grete and Rip were eating dust in the drag. "Are you trying to avoid me?" she asked, crowding her horse in alongside Grete's dun.

He pushed on a few strides, dragging his rope and not answering. "Because if you are," she said with eyes glinting, "I don't like it. We're equal partners in this. I want to know where we're going. I want to know what your plans are."

"Is that all?" he said bleakly.

"How much farther to your place is it?"

"If these mares hadn't gone lame we'd be there tonight—barring accidents."

She looked at him sharply. "What kind of accidents?"

Grete shrugged. "Crotton's got a tough crew and we're on his range." He remembered Rip then and raked a willful look at him. "Get up ahead," he growled.

Sary's tone was insistent. "Isn't Crotton

the one you used to be boss for?" When he nodded she said. "Did we have to come this way?"

"No. We could have spent three days swinging around to come in from the west. Wouldn't have made any difference with him; we'd have still been on Swallowfork."

She looked at him grimly. "Our ranch is completely surrounded by Swallowfork?"

The conversation annoyed him. It showed and he was aware that it showed. "That's right," he said, and looked past her, eyes narrowing. He reined his horse out around her and, putting steel to its flanks, tore off at a run toward where, ahead of the drive, a couple of strangers had appeared, accosting Idaho. The gunfighter's lifted arm stopped the drive. Sary spurred after Grete, coming up with the group just as Ben pushed up on his black from where he had been riding swing. The newcomers turned wind-roughened faces, lifting scowling eyes, their attention at once twisting back to Grete. Beard-stubbled and brush-clawed they looked, Sary thought, like a pair of starved saddle tramps. Even their animals had this pinched, gaunted look.

"Alls I'm askin'," the nearer, taller one growled, "is your intentions. You've rounded up a crew an' you've got this jag of horses. Looks to me like you're fixin' to make a fight for that claim."

The other stranger nodded. This was a weedy slack-jawed man whose furtive eyes, a kind of washed-out gray, seemed unable to focus very long on anything. He rasped the jowls of his weak wrinkled face, bobbing his head again. "We're all out of pocket to that sonofabitch—don't be so damn stand-offish. Hell, it's all over town that you're back to—"

"Lally," Farraday said, "turn that bonerack around and start making tracks."

Lally's saddlemate said, "We've all got reasons whether you like 'em or not. Seems to me the best deal is for all of us to put our guns in one pile. No sense in bein' pigheaded. There's enough short-enders hidin' out in the brush—"

"I don't want your damned help! Now wheel that bronc and get out of here."

Sary, watching, saw a tide of ruddy color surge above the tall man's open-throated collar. "What—" Ben began, and was cut off by Farraday's snapped "Keep out of this!" Lally licked cracked lips in an excess of nervousness as Grete crowded the dun against the tall man's trembling animal. "I won't tell you again, Frobisher."

The tall man's eyes sought out and found every one of them in slow and careful scrutiny before he yanked his horse around. But this was not enough. Spleen twisted his malicious face and he yelled back across a shoulder, "You've had your chance—don't come cryin' around me when you git hurt!"

Sary watched them whip their bony mounts through the brush, dip into the wash, and clout away out of sight. Farraday tipped up his face toward the sun and gave Patch the sign that they would stop here for chuck. There were things in his look which confused and halfway frightened her; gnawed by doubt she watched him heavily come out of the saddle. He appeared to be of two minds and not satisfied with either. She watched the black sweep of his glance strike Rip. "Get up on that rim with your rifle!" His eyes found Olds. "Kid, you help cook."

Idaho was carefully putting together a smoke and she could hear Patch unscrambling the pots from his packs, making more noise than the task would seem to warrant. Barney Olds went into the wash hunting firewood; and she got off her horse, seeing Ben come down too and, beyond Ben, the Mexican's dark gaze watching Grete. And all of this time her sharpened thoughts kept scratching around the ugly edges of something.

She loosened the cinch, pulling off her mount's bridle, turning him loose that he might forage like the mares. Her glance, coming up, found Farraday's eyes. "Go ahead," he growled, "say it."

She didn't care for that look and shook her head at him, searching her mind, wondering if it were fear which held her back instead of foolish hope that after all she might be wrong.

Ben had no such dilemma. Suspicion was written all over him, punching up the sharp angles of a face that was bright with anger. There was no room in him for doubt, and the malice which would not let him alone now prodded him beyond the control of past experience. He saw only that here, delivered into his hands, was the man who at every turn had blocked his purpose.

He stepped toward Grete belligerently, his whole mind vengefully wrapped about the prospect of stripping this dog of all pretensions. It set up a heady excitement in him and a pale flickering of this telegraphed its warning through the clench of his fingers and the whites of his eyes. "So—" he cried, "it's a fight you been figuring on taking us into!" The lips writhed away from his teeth in a sneer. "The gun who was going to keep trouble away from us! Grete Farraday, the big—" That far he got. Grete's fist, coming out of the middle of nowhere, crashed into his face like a load of brick, shaking him out of his tracks,

132

unbalancing him. His arms flew out and he went staggering back and his legs couldn't catch his weight. He went down, wildly yelling.

He rolled, caught himself, and came up off his knees spitting teeth and blood. He looked at the blood and then he pulled his head up. "Man—I'm going to kill you!" he shouted, and launched himself at Farraday head-on, at the last instant catching hold of his gun and bringing the weapon up out of its holster. Grete ducked that swing and laid his weight against Hollis and beat the man across the head. Anger was in the tight scowl of his mouth; he jammed the heel of a palm into Ben's chin and shoved with all his fury. Hollis', stumbling, got tangled in his spurs and again went down, this time sprawling between the legs of Grete's horse which promptly let fly with both hind feet.

Ben rolled clear, arms hugged about his head. But he was slower getting up. There was shock in his look and he had lost his pistol. His hat was off and sweat darkly laced the disheveled edges of his hair. He touched tongue to broken lips and, lifting a leg, ripped the spur off its boot and came at Grete, rushing in from that bent-over crouch.

Farraday kicked the man in the shin, bringing a shout from him; and now, before Ben could surge out of his crouch, cracked a knee full into the man's twisted face. Ben's arms flew out. He drew one agonized breath and came all the way up to full height, wholly open.

It was Farraday's chance. But with fist drawn back Grete dropped the arm, stepping away from Ben. Mercy had nothing to do with this. It had no tie-up with the rest of the crew nor had it, directly at least, been inspired by the girl although, discovering the expression of distaste around her mouth, he realized her presence might unconsciously have influenced him. His glance squeezed down until only the full swell of her breasts remained in focus below the white blur of her face. He could not help this. She saw what was in him and he could not help that, either.

He dragged his look away from her, observing Idaho's rigidity, the yellow-gray shine of his unwinking regard. The others—Rip, Frijoles, and Patch—had no conscience in the matter. They would not have interfered this time; they would have let him kill Ben if that had been his intention.

This conviction narrowed his eyes, disturbing and confusing him; and Sary chose just then to loose some nearly imperceptible signal which, destroying the gunfighter's cocked readiness, worked through him like an acid, reflected in those small changes which touched his raw-red cheeks. Hollis, to the left of him, stood with all his weight heavily settled into spread legs. He dragged a smearing hand across his chin and, feeling the group's unspoken indifference, looked, almost blankly, around at them, too mentally spent to exhibit resentment.

Farraday said, "Let's get those mares moving," knowing that none of this yet had been settled, that each of these, in his own time if he could, would try to slide out with a few head or try to kill him.

Ben moved first, climbing into his saddle like a man half-asleep. Rip and the Mexican, tightening clinches, also swung up. The kid let go of his armload of wood, started to speak, changed his mind and went along toward the bay he'd left on dropped reins. Patch, swearing now, began to pack up.

All of this Grete saw. He heard Sary coming nearer but did not take his eyes off them even after she stopped until they were gone beyond pistol reach. Then he turned with considerable reluctance. He could not certainly discover her mood and stood stiffly, guard up, waiting.

"Is that true, what Ben said?"

"I told you there'd be trouble."

"But not that you were inviting it."

She saw his face tighten up. That unyielding stoniness was back in his look. Her lips, red as wolf's candle, smiled at him bitterly. "I had you figured right the first time—"

"You made the deal. You had your reasons."

"And what of that ranch I was supposed to get half of?"

"You'll get your half when I take it away from him!" He started to wheel, twisted back and said roughly: "You want to call this off?"

She stared, eyes widening, in the stillness of pure astonishment. She took a sudden deep breath and said, "No," inscrutably.

Farraday searched for tobacco, putting together a smoke, his somber glance making nothing of her expression. His hands grew clumsy and he pitched the thing away. She had a lot of control and this impressed him but his experience with women made him doubt her sincerity. He believed all women to be greatly accomplished at acting out whatever parts seemed most likely to further their desire of the moment. He had expected her to jump at the offer he'd just made.

"A woman," she said, "can be a realist too. Nothing is ever quite as bad as we think." After a moment she said, "What did you do to this Crotton?"

Farraday considered that. "Most of what he's got he took away from other people, a regrettable proportion of it with my help. Of course it's all public land. All he has is squatter's rights and so I asked him for a piece of it. When he turned me down I filed on it. When he got around to it he burned me out."

She studied his face, her own preoccupied, her eyes unfathomably intent, understanding how unlike him it must be to interpret himself to anyone. He was probably unaware of the extent to which his words had unmasked him. He was a forthright man, knowing little of the gentler aspects of living, or had submerged such knowledge in the driving need which he must have for motion. He would view life if he ever took the time to consider it at all, in terms of perpetual struggle; she had seen enough of him to know this, to realize how necessary turmoil had become to him.

She said, "What do you believe?" and saw the puzzled, half-irascible way it pulled his eyes around. "Is it your conviction you have as much right to Swallowfork as Crotton?"

"Not to Swallowfork, maybe, but to a particular piece of it." He thought about that, abruptly nodding. "Certainly."

"A brutal philosophy."

"It's a brutal land, Sary. You won't scare off wolves by dropping a handkerchief."

"If we've a right to the land surely the law is bound—"

"This isn't Texas. Have you any idea how big this county is? It runs from Road Forks, in New Mexico, straight west to the Granite Mountains, hardly a whoop and a holler from the California line. That's just the width of it—roughly five hundred miles. Except for Bisbee, Tombstone, Pierce, Willcox, and Ajo, which have marshals, all that country is policed by a sheriff, and the sheriff stays where the votes are—Tucson. There's your law."

136

"But surely there are deputies. . ."

"Deputy for these parts is Johnny Behan. Johnny's best friend around here is Curly Bill. Nobody will cry if we don't make it."

She shook her head. "I can't go along with that. You said most of this Swallowfork range was taken from others. Unless they've all quit the country those others have got a stake in this."

"You just saw a couple of them. Lally and Frobisher. If they had four legs," Grete said, "they'd rate with coyotes."

Sary looked a long while at him. "You're too hard on people. Isn't there any faith in you?"

"Sure." With his smile stretched thin and tough Grete slapped a hand against the butt of his pistol. "I've got a heap of faith in what this'll do for me."

FIFTEEN

For two interminable hours they slogged through the monstrous heat of Texas Canyon where every view, choked or cluttered, was distorted by an unrelieved glare refracted from the surface of the naked rock. It was more punishing than the roughs they had come through southeast of Bowie. It wasn't black malpais—which at least had not crucified dust-inflamed eyes—but a kind of buff granite in a weird profusion of crazily strewn boulders that, of infinite variety, ranged from chunks the size of a midget's head to mighty slabs that were huge as ships, some of these precariously balanced above the trail.

It was like crossing the bottom of some vanished sea. Prickly pear, occasional ocotillo brightly tipped with scarlet bloom, century plants with stalks thrust up like lances, Spanish dagger and yellowing yucca grew sparsely out of this barren soil with here and there among the rocks the incredibly twisted shapes of live oak, some of these hardly six feet tall and older, Grete said, than Balaam's ass.

The wrinkled air of this trough was like a breath from hell. The ground underfoot was decomposed granite, loose on top and fetlock-deep, abrasive as a rasp against the unshod hoofs of the mares. The drive by now was strung out over nearly half a mile, the limping animals whickering miserably, barely able to drag one bleeding foot after another. And nothing to be done—"unless," Grete told the protesting girl, "you can find some way of fashioning boots for them. Cloth's no good and we haven't got the metal or any way to shape it. It's going to have to be leather, and when we've got all the saddles cut up more than half this bunch will still be barefoot."

"But isn't there some other way we could take? You said—"

"Not from here; and it's not enough better to be worth two more days. We'll quit this stuff pretty quick. Eight more miles and we'll know what you've bit into."

"You mean we'll be at the claim?"

He sucked on a tooth and considered her grimly. "That's right," he said—"if Swallow-fork let's us get that far."

She peered across the jumbled rocks toward the heights, glance darkly haunted, and wiped some of the moisture away from her neck. "Grete, did you kill French?"

Instead of answering, he skreaked around in the saddle to look back over the drive.

She said impulsively, "I don't believe it. I know you're hard, but. . ." Her eyes searched his face. "It was Ben, wasn't it?"

"Whyever would you think that, Miz' Hollis?"

"He's that kind. We might as well face it. He'll do anything he can to drive you out or get you killed."

Grete's mouth squeezed thin. He looked at her carefully. If that was concern tramping through her voice it damn sure wasn't aroused over *him*. "Well, thanks," he said, "for the warning. If you know any prayers you better chouse them toward Idaho. Next time *he* tries somebody's liable to get planted."

On that note he left her, pushing the dun out ahead of the drive, bleakly eyeing the country separating where they were from where he intended to climb out of this canyon. It was all up and down, more than a plenty of it out of his sight, practically all of it suitable to ambush.

With Sary still in his head he wondered somewhat bitterly if any person ever really came to know another. Generally you saw what they put out for you to see; occasionally, with luck, you might scratch a little deeper, or something—usually an emotion—briefly pulled the veil aside. Frequently this was bad although some good might come of it. It was bad because a man was apt to read more into such glimpses than would eventually prove to have been there. Too often you saw what you wanted to see.

This was certainly no time to be having his mind on a woman. It was the place where a man had better take a good look at his hole card. Crotton would know by now that he was back and Crotton wasn't one to put trust in half-measures. When he struck it would be like an avalanche. He hadn't forgotten the Lallys and Frobishers or what they would do if he got led up an alley. He knew all about hate. He'd come down on this drive like a clap of thunder.

All of Grete's thinking heretofore had been filled with his own plans, with what he figured to do and how best to do it. He saw the truth now. Crotton wouldn't wait.

The man couldn't afford to. Grete should have seen this, should at least have worked up some alternate plan in the event prospective plans were, like now, no longer feasible. But all of Grete's figurings had been predicated in terms of Swallowfork's enemies, on the envy

140

and fury and bitter resentment Crotton had stirred up over the years. Grete unconsciously had been counting—as Stamper had realized—on the whole range being eventually pulled into it. He had visualized success as coming through a carefully integrated series of hit-and-run impacts which must pull Crotton down sure as God made little apples.

Now as he thought about it, he realized all of that was out. Crotton had been way ahead of him.

The man's only defense—and surely Crotton would have seen this—lay in hitting Grete fast with everything he had. To keep the rest of them off, to frighten them back into their subservient neutrality, he was bound to use Grete for a horrible example. He *had* to do this or all his past didos would rise up to engulf him.

Grete cursed his own blindness.

"Looks like that biscuit you're chompin' is plumb full of weevils," Idaho remarked, bending his horse in beside Grete. "You tryin' to kill these damn mares?"

Farraday scowled. He should have handled Frobisher different. He'd had the means within his grasp and had let whipped pride and arrogance bang the door on any aid he might have got from those King Crotton had humbled. A combine could have stood Crotton off, pecking away at the man, whittling his resources down chunk by chunk until, finally at bay, he was backed into a corner where their teeth could get at him. Now it was Grete who was bound for that corner and it was Stamper's talk which had turned him so proud.

"You better wake up," the gunfighter grumbled. "This stock's in bad shape. Been a dozen foals dropped in the last fifteen minutes. Right now," he said, whacking a boot with his rein ends, "the tail end of this drive is drug out for a mile."

Grete hardly heard him. All Grete's faculties were engaged in the frantic search to find some means of getting out of this trap he had dragged them all into.

Stroat—Felix Stroat, he remembered, was the fellow Crotton had lifted into that ramrod's job. Stroat was an old hand, utterly loyal. Small, whip-thin, intolerant of anything which stood against the brand, he had been in line for that top-pay job when Crotton had put Grete over him.

The man had taken Grete's orders but he had never quite managed to hide his resentment; Grete had sensed more than once the fury festering within. Multiplied by years it had become an ugliness, distorted—and here was Grete's risk; but there might still be one thin chance. The possibility stemmed from Stroat's character, from the compulsions which made Stroat do what he did . . . traits which might prove stronger than Stroat's unreasoning bitterness could manage.

The Crotton ramrod was a man who could not bear to destroy anything which, in Crotton's ownership, could be an asset to Swallowfork. Grete recalled how the man had once kidnapped a herd of cattle he'd been told to run over a cliff. This had worked out well for Crotton and should have fetched Stroat more than a straw boss' job but Crotton, picking Grete for foreman, had wanted a man who would carry out orders and ride roughshod over everything. Stroat must have taken a particular delight in burning Grete out. Still corroded with hate, Stroat would boss whatever Crotton did now.

If the man realized his weakness and stood against it they were licked. Grete had to gamble that Stroat would not, that his pride in possessions would in the last ditch prove stronger than any other need which might sway him.

This was where Grete was in his thinking when Idaho, graveled by his inattention, irascibly caught at Grete's reins, bringing both horses to a stop. "I say we've gone far enough—these mares has got to rest!"

"Get that paw off my reins."

The gunfighter finally took the hand away. His yellow-flecked eyes never left Grete's face. "I told you how it was going to be. You let that girl down—"

"She knows what the deal is."

"She don't know Crotton and that sonofabitch Stroat."

"I gave her a chance to pull out—"

"That girl thinks you're the right hand of God!" All the bleak frustration of the man's balked passion was in those words he flung so bitterly at Grete. "You're not foolin' me! You're out to make Crotton eat crow an' you got about as much chance as a fiddler in hell."

"You all through now?"

"You'll know when I'm through!"

"Then get on with it. That Swallowfork bunch—"

Idaho used every unsavory epithet he could lay a foul tongue to and Grete took it, hearing not the obscenity but the tortured cry of a soul on the rack. It might have been his past self to which Grete was listening, understanding at last how negligible had been the difference between them, discovering how many of the same wrong turns he'd known as intimately as Idaho. Proximity to Sary had worked its change in each of them. The gunfighter knew that it had come, for him, too late.

"I'm going through with this," Farraday said.

"By God, you can't! That bunch hits us now the way this stock's spread out—Christ, man, use your head! That kid might do what you tell him, but the rest of these tramps—"

"They can't stand against the both of us."

"I told you about that!"

"You'd let personal spite—"

"Jesus God, man! You think it'll help that girl to lose everything she's got? Those mares. . ."

The man's bitter eyes, leaping past Grete, went pale and wide, sick as though a knife had chunked into him. "Quiet," he growled. "She's comin'."

"Are you stopping here?" Sary asked, pulling up.

Grete with raised brows stared at Idaho.

The girl, plainly worried, looked at both of them, sensing tension. Idaho said, "Tell this fool to turn around!"

She considered Grete, her attention shifting to the gunfighter soberly. "I can't do that. It was a part of our agreement he should give the orders—"

"He's give 'em, girl. Look where we're at!"

A wind rushed down off the higher slopes and tugged at her shirtwaist, tumbling a lock of red hair across her cheek. She pushed it away, her eyes searching Grete.

He brought the dun up a step, trying to make out what lay behind this look, turned suddenly restless, not sure of anything. A deeper color crept into her cheeks and the lock of hair fanned across them again. He bent to catch a surer look, what he saw unsettling him badly. Idaho bawled in unbridled fury, "Get this drive turned around! You don't owe him a thing!"

"Grete, tell me the truth. Do we have any chance?"

He observed the contempt on the gunfighter's face and was still so long she put the question again.

There was a wicked gleam in Idaho's stare, a kill-crazy hate glaring through the jealous rage that was destroying his control. Grete realized one further thing, that if it came to crossing guns with him the man would get his shot off first. Grete was also swayed by the look which the girl, without reservation, had so recently shown him. He fought his bitter thoughts, fought the cold paralysis settling over him. "Be pretty risky . . . but I believe we have."

"Why, you damned hypothecator!" Idaho yelled. "All you want is to get even with that sonofabitch! She's the one that takes the risk—you got nothin' to lose but your miserable life!" His hand dropped and spread above the grip of his pistol.

"No!" Sary cried, ramming her horse in between them. Idaho had to use both hands to keep his rearing mount from going over. He clouted him viciously between the ears, laying into the horse with the butt of his quirt, hammering him down to a trembling stand.

He looked about ready to try it on Grete. "We can't make no fight with this stock spread to hell an' gone!"

"Nobody wants a fight," Grete told Sary— "not here anyway, not now," he said. He paid no attention to the gunfighter. In the man's present mood Grete knew if they swapped glances there would be blood spilled. He saw the girl's eyes change. "If we can keep them spread out, and if the crew—"

But Idaho had to work off his spleen. "If!"

he jeered, bony face thrust toward Grete. "If wishes was horses you'd have 'em all!" He spat and looked back at Sary. "I'd as soon go up against Geronimo's Apaches as to brace Crotton's bunch with their warpaint on! You listen to me—"

But she wanted to hear Grete. "You have a plan?"

"Well . . . not a plan exactly." Grete took in a deep breath. "If we keep on like we're going they'll ride us down one at a time. If we bunch up they bag the lot of us. What it boils down to—"

"You want to give it up?"

"It's not that. I'm going on—"

"Then let him go," an' good riddance!" That was Idaho, swelled up like a toad.

"There's a way," Grete said. "If it works we get our ranch."

"If there was a way," the gunfighter snarled, "he'd of taken it. He's workin' up now to tell you we got to ditch the stock. By God, you turn 'em loose it's the last you're goin' to see of 'em! Jesus God, ma'am, you let me—"

Sary spoke to Grete. "Do what you have to do. Never mind the mares—I never had any real right to them anyway. Ben got Tate's money. I got the bills. The bank and the merchants teamed up and got a judgment." Her eyes met Grete's straightly. "I was pretty bitter. The night before the sheriff was due Ben suggested we grab the mares and clear out. At the time it seemed like a good idea." She brushed the hair away again. "Go ahead and cut loose of them if—"

Idaho snapped, "Don't talk like a fool! You earned them horses. You put up with plenty. Olds has told me all about Tate and what he done for that bastard—excusin' your presence, ma'am. You got a right to anythin' you can git outa this." He glared malignantly at Grete. "I ain't lettin'. . ."

He wasn't reaching the girl. Her eyes were still on Farraday. The courage and pride and trust Grete saw in them made him feel mighty small. The gaunt one had a right to be riled. It made Grete sick to think how he had used this girl, looking out for his own, whip-sawing all of them, caring for nothing but his plans for smashing Crotton. For the first time he paused, actually stopping, to wonder if he ought to go on with this thing. But it was kind of a passing thought at best. They were deep into land claimed by Swallowfork now. Crotton—even if they wanted to—would never let them go. Sometimes a man could bluff, but not here. Crotton knew where they were; if not, he damned soon would know. They'd have to duck bullets every inch of the way. He said as much. Idaho cursed. "You git them mares—"

"Be still!" Sary said, and pushed her horse nearer Grete. She wondered if he truly understood how she felt. She wanted him to; there was only one thing in this world she wanted more. And that was to know how *he* felt, to be convinced that she was important to him. All the rest—the ranch, these horses, meant less than nothing; but she could not put the words in his mouth. "Well, Grete?"

"I'm going on."

He might have said a lot more, perhaps he should have; but he was seeing some things clearer now. He had finally come face to face with himself and some of his discoveries were starkly disturbing. There was confusion inside him and the shock of broken images, a strange uncomforting humility laced with shards of doubt. He managed to keep this off his face but he could not saddle her or any woman with the responsibility for what he meant to do. "I'm going to try it," he told Idaho.

A gun jumped into the gaunt man's hand.

SIXTEEN

They stared at each other, eyes bright and hard. The quiet had the feel of a watch wound too far.

Sary's cheeks turned white. She could not breathe. The hammer of the gun came back to full cock. Idaho softly said, "We'll see. . ." and Patch, coming up, growled, "What're we stopped for?"

"Resting the mares," Grete said through his teeth. "Break out some grub."

Cook saw the gun then. The lump bobbed in his throat. Sary, coolly knowing what chance she took, exactly backed her horse until her waist was between the gun's muzzle and Grete's chest. She said, ".'He's not going to shoot," and made her mouth smile for Patch. "Go along and get supper—and hurry it up, will you?"

She reached out for Grete's arm, pulling at its stiffness, feeling how furiously angry he'd become. She kept grim hold of him, fearfully turning, compelling him to turn, not giving him a chance to be quixotically foolish which she knew was what he felt bound to do, being a man and filled with purely crazy notions. Better to have him shamed than shot.

She didn't dark risk a look in Idaho's direction but she did out of the corners of her eyes catch a glimpse of the ludicrously gaping face of Patch. She got Grete turned around but that was all—she couldn't get him away from there. He grabbed the dun hard with both knees, anchoring the horse against the pull of her. She stopped too, rather than turn loose of him.

She saw the swollen veins in his neck as he twisted his head to glare over a shoulder. She was suddenly frightened what he might say would trigger the gun in spite of everything. "Go on," she cried bitterly, "get yourself killed! If your damned pride means—"

"I'll take care of my pride!" He said gruffly to cook, "When you go back pass the word to the boys to watch sharp for Swallowfork. They're going to come down on us. First puff of gunsmoke I want the boys running. You got that?"

Patch nodded.

"Never mind the mares. I don't want no one stopping to swap lead with that bunch. At the first sign of trouble light out and keep going."

Patch dubiously looked at the girl, then at Idaho. The gunfighter had scowlingly lowered his pistol. In spite of what Sary's intervention must have done to him he began to show interest. His glance was sharp. "Let me git this straight. You're wantin' Crotton's gunnies to figure the crew's run out an' took of for Texas?"

"That's the general idea."

Contempt came into the gaunt man's look. "If I know them rats they'll sure as hell do it."

"Not without you let them," Grete said. "You been shooting off your jaw about Sary's interests ever since I got into this deal. Put up or shut up."

The gunfighter's cheeks showed a rawer red. His mouth tightened. But after a moment he tipped a curt nod and a grin wryly streaked across his scabbed lips. He shoved his gun back in leather. "What do you want 'em to do?"

Grete wasn't sure at all how far he could trust the man. His eyes were too guarded to be certainly read. "Take them up the north slope quick as you're out of Crotton's sight and wait in the rocks beyond the rim till I come up with you."

Idaho's eyes watched him, then shifted to Patch. "What the hell are you waitin' for?"

"I want a plain order—"

"You got one. Git goin'."

Cook's head swung to Crete. "You're still wantin' grub?"

"I want to butcher a little time. Might as well be putting it away."

Patch turned his horse and rode off.

"What about Sary?" the gunfighter asked.

"She stays with the horses." Grete saw the anger leaping through his cheeks. "She'll be safe enough. I know this country and I know Crotton's crew. They're not going to bother any stranded woman. Crotton, so far as women are concerned. . ." He caught the skeptical climb of the gaunt man's brows. "You can take my word for it."

Idaho's lip started to lift but he flattened it out when he saw the girl take her hand off Grete's arm. He picked up his reins, face inscrutable again. "What about the horses?"

"They're not going to run, the shape their feet are in. Anyway Crotton's boss, Felix Stroat, ain't the kind to play hell with a stock of top blood mares. He'll take care of those e-quines fine as silk."

"That's what you're countin' on?"

"I'm putting a big stack on it." Grete wheeled the dun, heading back; Sary, following, appeared now almost as wooden-faced as the gunfighter.

Idaho moved his horse up beside Grete.

151

"This Stroat a particular friend of yours?"

Farraday looked at him coldly and laughed.

"That's no answer!" the gunfighter snarled.

"If I was about to fall over he'd give me a push."

Idaho's stare narrowed down. "Then he'll be after us with everything he's got."

"That's why I'm dropping the mares. It would go against his grain to let that stock get so much as a hair mussed. Time he wakes up we're going to be out of this jackpot." Grete, swinging wide, cut over to say to Rip, "You understand what you're to do when they hit?"

The man glared at him, finally nodding.

"All right. Go up there a ways where you can see around that bend. Not knowing how far we'll have got with these mares, they'll probably be coming right down the canyon. Just before they get within good killing range, let off that rifle and bust for the stock. That's to suck them down here and to tip off our boys. You'll have farther to run because you're going to come pounding straight up to the mares—that's to make sure they see what we've got here."

"When they comin'?"

"They won't be far away now. You see the rest of us fading, you let out a yell and come busting right after us. I'll see that you draw double pay for today."

"I ain't drawn *no* pay yet," Rip scowled. "They been holdin' it back to make sure we stick." His look said that wouldn't stop him if things got rough.

Grete nodded and turned back, throwing a look overhead. It would have done no good to have promised the man more. Loyalty was something you just couldn't buy. He looked down where the mares were cropping dried grass; in spite of everything, he thought, they made a mighty pretty sight. There were more foals now. He reckoned upwards of fifty. That brought out his tight grin.

Sary had gone on—he caught occasional glimpses of her, moving among the mares and boulders, following Patch along the route toward the drag. Grete saw a thin curl of smoke where the kid was already pulling the packs off the work stock. Idaho was waiting.

Grete slanched another thoughtful squint at the sun, heeled well over, throwing out longer, deeper shadows where rocks stood up in its path. In about another hour this particular stretch was going to be hard to see well in. Crotton would know this. So would Stroat. No telling if the pair were together. Crotton could be home. He could be perambulating about in town where folks could afterwards remember they had seen him.

Idaho said, breaking into Grete's conjectures, "What'd you mean, 'time he finally wakes up'?"

"Hmm? Oh—Stroat." The sun struck up a little flash from Grete's teeth. "They'll be looking for us to run these horses up into the mountains to push them onto my claim. They don't mean to let us—you can understand that. What you don't know about is Stroat, the way he feels about livestock. So we drop these horses right into his lap; he hasn't figured on that, it throws his whole schedule off. Whle he's playing around with these mares and their foals we're on our way to Crotton's headquarters. Time he wakes up he's got this stock on his hands. He can't let go of them; he'll have to split up his crew. We'll be sitting behind walls time those buggers catch up with us."

The gunfighter said grudgingly, "All right. You've sold it to me. But that don't change

153

nothin' else that's between us."

The rash of Rip's rifle flung its cascading echoes across the drive's stopped sprawl from a hundred different rock faces. Its muzzle burst was a lurid flash through the gloom of piled-up shadows, driving Farraday, the girl, and the bony-faced gunfighter out of the wavering light from Patch's fire. Those three were alone there, cook and Olds having gone up the line with hot food and java. This seemed to be working out just about the way Grete had figured; and now a wild racket of hoofs drumming toward them from where Rip had triggered the warning sent Grete and Idaho up into leather.

The gunfighter's yell tore off through the trumpeting call of the stallion and he whirled, holding his mount, as the crew thundered past with every evidence of panic. Grete saw gun flashes blossom where Rip had stood sentinel and saw the man, nearer, twist around to fire back.

Leaning down, Grete hollered at the girl: "Remember! Stay right where you are! Patch some more wood on that fire so they can see you—act trapped, like you can't find a horse—don't know where to turn next." Staring into her white face he had a moment of misgiving; then he pulled back into the saddle. "You'll be all right," he said gruffly, and spun the horse to find Rip, forty yards away, lashing his mount straight up the north slope.

Idaho, back of Grete, cut loose without compunction, emptying his rifle, snarling when Rip kept going. The rocks hurled back the racket with a hundred raucous voices and the mares pretty near went crazy; Grete could see their black shapes—some with foals desperately trying to stay at their sides—rushing every whichway, neighing and squealing, some of them kicking. He saw one foal going end over end.

Rip, bent low, suddenly topped out over the rim and muzzle lights winked through the roaring black as Grete, spurring away from the last touch of fireglow, caught up with the gunfighter's cursing.

"Never mind," he called; "anyone's liable to lose their head—"

"Three of 'em!" Idaho shouted. "Three is all that went by me! Rip makes four—where's the other?"

"You sure?"

"By God you'll see!"

Grete, remembering the hating half-defiant way Rip had stared when he'd offered to double the man's wages, knew the fellow had "rolled his cotton'" as they'd have said back in Texas. And now there was another gone. which of the remainder would show up to be counted? None of them probably if they could manage to get clear.

The gunfighter yelled, "Want to turn up here?"

Grete looked back and couldn't even find the fire. "All right." He cut the dun over. Putting him up that sharp incline he thought more than once to hear somebody back of them but didn't see anything. He was glad he was using a double-girthed hull. Twisting around some of those slabs, the leathers skreaked and popped like pistols.

When they rimmed out he pulled up, peering back. "What's ailin' you?" Idaho said. Grete held a hand up. Both of them listened but the men up ahead were making such a clatter going through rocks and brush Grete couldn't be sure if he heard anything or not. The pitch looked black as a stack of stove lids. Squirming around he found the gleam of the fire, not bright like it had been, a huddle of horsebackers milling about it. He shook his head. "Nerves, I reckon." It was a concession he normally would not have made.

"Better git on," the gunfighter said, " 'fore we lose 'em."

They struck off through the dark, both horses heaving. They came up with the others. Grete said, "We'll rest a bit." He saw the hard set of the gunfighter's shoulders. "We're back far enough," he nodded. "Go ahead."

Idaho struck a match in cupped palms. Patch's grumpy scowl came out of the darkness, the Mexican's steeple-crowned hat, the kid's face. Idaho's bitter eyes came around. Patch cursed. "Now you know."

Grete, sighing said, "He could have been hit," but none of them believed it. He didn't himself. Ben wasn't the kind to be hit. He was a hitter.

"God damn it," Patch said, "we better give this thing up."

They sat there a moment. The kid tipped his head back. "Maybe that's him now."

They all heard the hoofs of an approaching horse moving erratically toward them. Not cropping grass, Grete thought; there's somebody on him.

Confused, or trying to be cautious maybe. Could be one of Crotton's Swallowfork bunch.

Patch slipped a gun out. Barney, next to him, caught Patch's wrist. "Hold it."

"Grete . . .?" a voice called tentatively. Idaho's face jerked. Behind him Frijoles softly let out his breath.

"Over here—around the rock," Grete said.

Dark as it was her eyes picked him out.

156

"Never mind. No point in my staying. Ben's sold you out."

Somewhere in the night's sudden quiet a shod and careless hoof struck rock. Frijoles, looking around nervously, crossed himself. "He's split them up," Patch said. "They're comin' after us."

SEVENTEEN

Grete told himself he should have known better than try to brace Swallowfork with this kind of crew—and it wasn't as though he hadn't been warned. He hated to be put in the position of promising something he wasn't going to be able to deliver. He had promised her half of a ranch, and it hacked him.

"They won't know where we are. . ." That was Barney, worriedly whispering the hope of at least three of them.

Grete was conscious of Sary's eyes. "Maybe not," he said gruffly, "but they'll know where we're headed." It wouldn't have been quite so mean if the girl had stayed with the horses; that would have forced Stroat to leave dependable men.

He rubbed a damp hand across his thigh, bitterly knowing there was no way of going back, of undoing what was done. He had either to give up the whole deal right here or get these dogs to Swallowfork pronto. And without he wanted a bullet in his back it would have to be their own choice that took them.

You could smell their fright—even the kid was panicked.

In their desperate reflections Crotton's headquarters was the mouth of the lion. How could he put them into it? How could he convince them their only chance for survival lay in doing the thing least likely to insure it?

Somehow it was the girl—Sary's continued regard—that shaped the empty gesture he hauled full-blown from the darker recesses of his need. He said, "If one of them stumbles into us now we'll have no chance at all, that's sure. I won't hold you boys—duck out if you've a mind to. I won't say you can get through but you can try. It's not over a hundred miles to the border. Go ahead. Good luck to you."

He sat back against the high swell of his cantle as though he had all the time in the world.

He could feel them fidgeting, could see the heavier black of them hanging there, free to go yet afraid to move. It was Patch who asked suspiciously, "And what'll *you* be doing?"

"What I set out to do," Grete said—"riding over to Crotton's ranch."

"With the girl?"

"If that's what she wants to do I won't stop her."

He had a feeling that Sary saw through what he was up to, that it was one more count against him with her; but she said cool enough, "Of course I'm going with you," and Idaho said, "You can count me in."

Barney Olds sighed. "Me, too."

"Hell," Patch said then, "what are we waitin' for?"

But Frijoles, Ben's man from the start, was still thinking. "Eef they have gone by us—"

"You're a free agent, Beans," Grete cut in. "If it's your notion you'd be better off by yourself then that's how you ought to play it. I don't want anyone along who'd rather be somewhere else."

The skies should have fallen after delivering

himself of that one. He felt Idaho's sharp look but squeezed the dun with his knees, swinging off toward the north at a circumspect walk, not daring to turn his head. Do it right, he told himself. Do it right or you'll never get there.

At least some of them were coming. He could hear the rasp of leather, a myriad of lesser sounds not exactly definable. In his mind he turned over the words of the Mexican, darkly wondering. If Crotton's bunch had gone past this might get pretty rough. But, knowing Stroat as he did, he did not consider it too likely. The man was too dogged, too methodically thorough, to risk overrunning his great opportunity. At least a fourth of his crew would have been left with the captured horses if only to make certain Grete had no chance to pull a rabbit out of the hat. Stroat, as Grete's *segundo*, had had plenty of experience with Grete's flair for legerdemain. Hollis, to be sure, would have told Crotton's ramrod of Grete's order to abandon the mares, but Stroat wasn't the kind to consider anything a fact without he had personally established it. He'd have the rest of Crotton's hired toughs spread out, beating the rocks and brush above the rim.

Knowing that any attempt here at haste would prove the surest means of attracting trouble, Grete was holding the pace to an exasperating walk, breaking it up now and again with short pauses—almost, Idaho crossly muttered, as though they were helping Stroat's Swallowforkers search.

This was the impression Grete was endeavoring to create, for only by such a frustrating device could he find any hope of digging themselves clear. Rip's flight over the rim in plain hearing of Stroat's crew, followed

160

by Ben's defection, had put Crotton's riders on their trail far too soon for Grete to consider any straight-out dash. The last thing he wanted was to make a race of this trip; he would have to find enough when they got there to get up the field pieces. If he were denied such a margin, Stroat's superior numbers could be made to tell heavily.

Grete's party had not gone a quarter of a mile when out of the gloom directly ahead of them somebody cursed. Grete, snapping his quick glance over his shoulder, discovered no one had quit him; but he saw also they had got too closely bunched. His yanked-back look found nothing in front of him to put a gun on. His horse had stopped—so had the rest of them. In this intensity of quiet the metallic sound of Idaho's leveraction repeater lifting a .44-.40 into firing position was about as restful as a Comanche war cry.

"You goddamn fools!" Stroat's voice ripped at them. "I told you, Haines—"

Everything appeared to happen at once then. Grete's eyes found the man and he grabbed at his sixshooter. He bent low over the horn and gouged the dun with his spurs. Idaho's Henry cracked spitefully—spoke again; but Stroat's horse was already in motion, flame spitting above the line of its plunge. Someone yelled behind Grete and Stroat disappeared between rocks as Grete triggered futilely and Idaho riddled the night with his rifle. "Come on—come on!" Grete shouted through the uproar, and drove the dun at full speed dead ahead.

Yells and cursing came through the rush of hoofs behind him and he held the big horse to its panicked run for another couple minutes before easing him into a more conservative gallop. The black shapes of the others were coming hard at his heels; then the girl thrust alongside. "We've got to stop—Barney's hurt!"

"He'll have to wait," Grete answered.

"Then you'll have to slow down or he isn't going to make it."

Grete, throwing a hand out to warn the rest of them, pulled up.

Patch was holding the kid in his saddle. "Where'd it catch you?"

Olds said, groaning, "In the chest—I'm all blood. You—you fellers go on."

Grete crowded the dun against the kid's horse and felt of him. He didn't need any light. He pulled off Olds' neckerchief and, folding it for padding, thrust it inside his shirt. Then he got the kid's belt and strapped the pad in place. "Tie him into his saddle," he told Frijoles; and Idaho's rifle began laying flat smashes of sound through the night. Sary cried at Grete: "What good will it do to go to Crotton's headquarters?"

"We can't make a stand here!"

"*Seguro*," growled the Mexican. And Patch said, "We got him anchored."

Grete led them off through a jumble of boulders, the girl hanging onto the reins of Barney's horse. There was a renewed burst of firing from Crotton's outfit. Lead smashed and flattened against the rocks, some of it squealing in wild ricochet. "Sharp pitch here," Grete warned and dropped from sight, the others following.

Ten minutes later they were climbing again. Grete, dropping back, leaned out to stare at the kid.

"None of it," Sary said, "is worth that boy's life!" Grete felt the searching look she threw at him. "Why are we going to Swallowfork?"

"We're going to Swallowfork because that is where we have to go to put a stop to this."

"And how do you propose to manage that?"

"Mostly what we do is going to depend on how things shape there. If Crotton's in town we'll fire the big house. That'll reach a long ways in a night black as this one, and it will give us some light. We'll take over the outbuildings. When Stroat's bunch comes in we'll drop what we can of them. What Stroat brings will be hired guns—the Swallowfork hardcases. Hurt those rannies bad enough and what's left will go straight over the hill."

"That's a pretty brutal outlook."

"What do you suppose Crotton sent Stroat to do? Hand down the Ten Commandments?"

Her face tipped around. "What other people do—"

"Don't give me that! We're not dealing with Bible tracts. When you set to fight wolves you've got to bite like a wolf bites."

"And what if they get there before we do?"

"Crotton will give out a story and that will be the end of it. He'll say it was tough about that woman but. . ."

Idaho pushed up. "I thought you said—"

"That was back there. Where I told her to stay!"

He lifted the dun into a lope again. They crested a ridge and there were ranch lights ahead of them—Crotton's headquarters, still a couple of miles off. Now the going was easier, gently rolling. They were out of the rocks and there was no brush here. Grete thought of the kid with a long regret, understanding this ride would be doing him no good and bitterly aware

163

that there was no help for it. More than Grete's inclination was involved; to have stopped would have been giving death warrants for all of them, and despite the harsh words he'd just flung at the gunfighter Grete did expect to reach the ranch first.

Crotton's crew, if Crotton was with them, may have by-passed this outfit and be waiting right now, but Grete did not believe this. He was gambling Stroat had charge of that bunch and he was gambling on what he knew of Stroat's character.

"When we ride in, spread out," he said over his shoulder. "We're not like to have any great amount of time. Every move's got to count. Watch the yard. Those lights don't signify —they're always turned up; Leppy, Crotton's cook, takes care of them. I'll fire the house. Rest of you scatter. Take cover in the outbuildings."

Idaho said, brushing alongside once more, "Could be trouble in that house. I'll go with you."

Grete slammed a look at him. "Why don't you say it?"

"Well, by God, I will! I never been sold out but there's always a first time. Way you've set this up it's got all the earmarks—"

"If it's a trap," Grete snarled, "it will close on me, too."

"That's what I aim to make sure of. You pick the house for yourself and send the rest of us into them outbuildin's. For all we know you've never quit Crotton—that bunch played around back there one hell of a while!"

Grete was too hacked to say anything to that. He clipped his horse with the steel again, sent him down the last stretch at a headlong gallop, pulling away from the others, so furious mad he would have tackled right then Crotton's whole crew single-handed.

But he got hold of his temper before he'd gone very far, this innate sense of the fitness of things reluctantly convincing him that, in Idaho's place, he might have felt the same way. It came to him then if he wasn't damned careful he might very well be bracing Swallowfork single-handed—"solo" as they said in this country.

Key to the man was in the gunfighter's stake and, viewed in that light, he threw a pretty long shadow. He had no stake in what they were doing here. Idaho's interest was centered in the girl and he was stringing along purely to make sure she didn't wind up grabbing the burnt end of things.

This didn't leave Grete much ground to stand on. It reduced his outrage to frying size, left him feeling about as tall as a toothpick. He wondered if this was how Sary saw him.

With mouth sucked in he checked the dun's lick to let the others come up. Hating this like poison, yet impelled to do it, he declared, facing Idaho squarely: "This don't change anything that's between us but I reckon you had some right to say that."

Grete couldn't own up that events in these last few hours had managed to turn the whole deal sour on him, that except for the girl he would dropped the damned business, that he was here now mainly to make good if he could on that brag of a ranch which had pulled Sary into it. Stamper's words, though he didn't suspect this, had got deeper under his hide than was apparent.

Idaho just stared at him, not saying anything. Grete had not aimed to go so far but now, grinding his pride into doll rags, said, "I'd be considerably favored if you *would* go with me."

The gunfighter's suspicion looked to grow progressively stronger. Grete was beginning to get a bit panicky under Idaho's hard and continuing attention when Sary said impatiently, "This boy's in a bad way. We've got to get him out of that saddle."

They'd drawn up at the edge of the yard and Grete, checking appearances against remembered knowledge of this place, jerked the girl a stiff nod. "Take care of him, ma'am—Frijoles can help. That boy has sure won his spurs on this trip. You just ride straight into that barn with him." They were in the deep dark of a bunch of old cottonwoods. "You hole up in the forge shed, Patch—that's it over there," he pointed; and brought his glance back to Idaho. "Ready?"

"This place is too quiet." The man's tone didn't like it.

"Cook's probably lit out. Crew is with Stroat, what he hasn't split off to look out for those mares." He threw another look around. "Likely Crotton's in town." A horse nickered tentatively from an open-face corral. "Listen—" Patch said, putting a hand out.

The rumor of travel was strong-lifting pulse. "That's them!" someone cried in a voice turned jumpy with nervous excitement. They all twisted around to stare hard into darkness. "Man, they're comin'!" cook said.

Grete tipped his head at the gunfighter. "Let's go."

They put their horses across the yard, flashing through bars of light from the house's open windows, the told-off trio striking diagonally toward the barn, Grete and Idaho making for the pillared gallery. Grete saw one dark room facing onto the yard which, thinking back, he was certain had just a moment ago been lighted. Quick fear splintered through the shell of his mind and a warning shout rushed out of his mouth. But the damage was done, his cry too late. The gunfighter's stare was like a curse as he reeled, missing his grab, and fell out of the saddle.

The gun barked again, cuffing the night with its sound, its muzzle flash striking like a lance from the blackness even as Grete, still gripping his rifle, flung himself off the dun. He struck limp and wildly rolled, saddle gun hugged against his chest, the crazy tightness in his head throwing him onto his feet in a crouching run, driving him across the pounding planks straight at the window.

He squeezed off his single shot with the snout of his rifle almost touching the sash, the black-powder flare briefly showing him Crotton's face. He bitterly knew that he had missed and cast the useless weapon aside. There was now only solid blackness in that room, for the door had been closed to keep out the light, but Grete knew that somewhere in this dark Crotton waited.

There was sweat in his palms, his heart was thumping when he wiped them across the canvas of his pants. He caught the pistol up out of its leather and, writhingly remembering Idaho's last look, cleared the sill in one dive that took him deep into blackness, piling him up in bleak shock against unyielding wood that shouldn't have been there. A gun battered the room with the wild fists of its racket, the rip and slap of those slugs nearly turning Grete crazy. He couldn't find his pistol but the search of his hands told him what he'd run into was Crotton's desk moved out of its corner. He dragged himself around it by pure animal instinct and, back of it, pulled himself onto his feet, feeling the stickiness of blood as he stood braced there hunting for Crotton with eyes that burned and watered trying to see through that acrid stench.

Either Crotton had shot his gun empty or was holding his fire till he had something to shoot at. If the man had reloaded Grete hadn't heard him, but he now heard the pounding of guns outside and knew that time wouldn't wait for him. Time was Crotton's friend; and any man slick enough to have planted this desk in the path from that window would have been smart enough to have a couple of extra guns. He wouldn't have to reload, and any moment now some of that bunch who had come back here with Stroat were like to bulge into this room hunting cover. Grete's dug-in guns, by the sound, were still holding, but without benefit of crossfire it could be only a matter of minutes before Stroat's superior numbers engulfed and silenced them. Stroat's voice came over the yard to him now, cold, dispassionate, dry as stove wood.

There were spurs on Grete's heels that he would have to get rid of before he dared risk any attempt at changed placement. If he did not break out of this situation soon . . . He was driven to thought of rushing Crotton but gave this up, having no faith in miracles.

He found it hard to bend over without losing his balance, but someway managed, catching hold of the rowels and worrying the leathers. They finally came loose and it looked for a moment like he was not going to get back up. When he got up he was filled with dizziness, freezing to the desk with his empty right hand—he had the spurs in the other. He knew where the door was but he did not know if he could get there.

A sudden racket of boots crossed the floor of the gallery. Grete heard them pause outside the window. Forced back on the oldest trick in the deck he flung both spurs at the wall he had come through, straightaway charging across the room, deafened by Crotton's firing. His legs, stumbling over a chair, pitched him headlong. The continued grunt of Crotton's slugs smashed wood all around him. The fellow on the gallery got into it too, most of his lead drumming into the desk.

On his knees Grete snatched up a part of the chair, hurling it at the flash of Crotton's pistol. Crotton yelled as Grete lunged for the door. Grete went through falling, rolling frantically away from that bright threshold and the stretch beyond it that was in Crotton's sight. Doubled over with pain he tried to push himself up, hearing boots coming after him, knowing he wasn't going to make it. His muscles seemed to have got uncoupled, the line of command from his will severed someway. He got a leg under him, catching hold of a table and—seeing the lighted lamp that was on it—sending it toppling, childishly pleased with the lurid blaze that sprang up. Crotton's shape filled the doorway, savagely swearing.

The man could see Grete's hands were empty but he had never been one to throw away an edge and would not now. Grete laughed in his face. "You'll never hear me beg and you'll never get back to where you were in this country. Go ahead and shoot."

"God damn you!" Crotton snarled and tipped up his pistol: but he never pulled the trigger. A gun cracked once behind him, the roar of it bending the leaping flames that now were running like mad across the floor. Crotton's eyes dilated. His whole shape stiffened. He staggered a quarter-way round and collapsed.

Idaho, gray-cheeked and bloody, stepped over him. "Jesus God, man—" he gasped, "we've got to get out of here!"

He thrust down his left hand, hauling Grete to his feet. "Sling your arm about my neck. We're goin' to show a few jaspers we ain't trimmed yet—"

"Wait a minute," Grete said, and bent and picked up Crotton's pistol. He saw that it was fully loaded.

"They're gettin' ready," Idaho said, "to rush the barn. We better git out there."

A rush of feeling tightened Grete's throat but he had no way of unlocking the words. He gripped Idaho's shoulder—hard. The man grunted, "We're goin' to play hell gittin' back through that winder."

This was the room, now swirling with smoke, in which Crotton had been accustomed to entertain those who came to court his forebearance. It was elegantly appointed, lavishly furnished; none of this mattered to Grete or the gunfighter. All they wanted was to get out of it before Stroat's crew rushed the suddenly silent barn. The same gnawing fear wrenched at both of them.

Directly across the room as they now stood was a door leading, as Grete knew, into other parts of the house. The main entrance to the house was on their left, hung with stra-iron hinges. There was too much fire between them and this, but only one bad spot keeping them away from the other. "Let's get at it," Grete said. He slid his left arm over the gunfighter's shoulder, Idaho's right solidly clamping about Grete's waist. In this manner, sideways, they stumbled, gasping, into a hall, Idaho almost lugging him until he got some of the smoke coughed out of his lungs.

The left leg of Grete's pants below the knee was smoldering. The gunfighter's shirt showed several burned places, one of these still glowing. "Pull over," he growled as they came into the kitchen. Grete would have ignored this in his haste to quit the place, in the reproach of his concern for Sary Hollis, but the gunfighter's stubborn weight was not to be denied. It took them to the sink where he pumped a bucket of water, sloshing it over Grete's clothes, then up-ending once over himself. "Never hankered," he muttered, "to bein' took for no damned lightnin'-struck tree."

Grete got the back door open, Idaho breaking the lamp with his gun-barrel. Grete, burning up with impatience, saw that the near end of the barn wasn't over a hundred feet away, but between them and it was a spring wagon with the shapes of three men watching the barn from the house side of it. When the lamp went out the nearer man jerked a look over his shoulder. He let out a yell and, backing into the fellow next to him, brought his rifle up and around. Idaho shot him. The middle man got off two rounds from his shooter before Grete knocked him in a heap with a leg hit. The other jigger, rattled, tried to get around the wagon and ran head-on into a slug from the barn.

"Watch it," growled the gunfighter as Grete after the manner of a man in his cups began to flounder toward the wagon. "Give a broken-backed sidewinder a good enough chaw an' he'll git you just as—"

"I've got to—"

"Here they come!" yelled Idaho, running toward the corner of the house. The elongated shadows of the Swallowfork pack, driven forward by the flames, raced over the yard, cavorting like devils across the boards of the barn. Only one gun showed its muzzle wink there as Grete stumbled after him gripping the repeater dropped by the first man downed at the wagon.

Idaho had stopped just short of the yard, crouching there, waiting for something to throw his lead at. Grete, too, pulled up now, locking rimless lips against the pain that clawed through him, fighting the nausea and fear that had hold of him, trying to shut out the pictures that crowded his mind. *Only one answering gun left inside that barn.*

No shouts, no jeers, no crazy running marked the mopping-up tactics of Stroat's advance across the yard. By the look of those shadows he had his men spread well apart, but they were moving inexorably nearer, battering the barn with a steady fire. If anyone still lived inside those walls. . .

Idaho's pistol, wickedly cracking, fetched up Grete's rifle at the fanned-out line of Swallowfork gunmen moved into wavering sight beyond the corner of the kitchen wing. Grete saw one pitch flat on his face, another one staggered; farther over in the flickering flame-splattered dark a third Swallowforker spun, clutching himself. Another fellow's whipped-around face loosed a frantic yell as Grete squeezed off the first shot from his captured Henry. The yeller toppled.

"Get that pair," Stroat said dry as dust.

Grete abruptly found his face in the dirt. But he still had the rifle and now, squirming around in bitter disgust at the circumscribed status of his own activity, he lined its sights on the nearest of Crotton's bully boys and dropped him. Three more immediately crumpled just beyond this fellow. Panic hit the rest as a ragged yell broke out of the muzzle-rimmed murk along their far flank. Powder rings blossomed all across that side of the yard. Stroat's crew, demoralized, deserted him right then, each man striking out for himself, running blindly, some in their fright even dropping their rifles. One panicked walloper loped straight at Idaho who, caught with an empty pistol, hurled the useless weapon completely missing him. For one stark instant a pillar of leaping flame, rocketing skyward from the collapsed roof of Crotton's office, garishly illuminated Ben Hollis' twisted features. Grete's shot took the man between the eyes, killing him instantly.

That suddenly it was over. Squatters and dispossessed ranchers led by Lally and Frobisher made short work of what was left of Crotton's gunhands. Stroat and three others caught with emptied weapons were straight-away hanged from the hay hoist. It was Sary who told Grete after the doc had gone off to patch up some of the others that Barney Olds was going to make it. Patch was dead and Frijoles, too. Some of the townsmen, led by Stamper, had gone after the mares. The Lally and Frobisher adherents were squabbling now over which was to get what part of Crotton's range. "But Lally has promised you can have those springs, and Idaho says he'll get over there right away to. . ."

She saw that Grete wanted to say something. He didn't have the strength to explain all that was in his mind but, catching hold of one of her hands, he did manage to get out the part

173

that most mattered. And Idaho, bumping Grete's shoulder with a careful fist, said, "What I told him before still goes. He better take good care of you."

MORE HARD-RIDING, STRAIGHT-SHOOTING WESTERN ADVENTURE FROM LEISURE BOOKS

Make the Most of Your Leisure Time
with
LEISURE BOOKS

Please send me the following titles:

Quantity	Book Number	Price

If out of stock on any of the above titles, please send me the alternate title(s) listed below:

Postage & Handling

Total Enclosed $

☐ Please send me a free catalog.

NAME _____
(please print)

ADDRESS _____

CITY _____ STATE _____ ZIP _____

Please include $1.00 shipping and handling for the first book ordered and 25¢ for each book thereafter in the same order. All orders are shipped within approximately 4 weeks via postal service book rate. PAYMENT MUST ACCOMPANY ALL ORDERS.*

*Canadian orders must be paid in US dollars payable through a New York banking facility.

Mail coupon to: **Dorchester Publishing Co., Inc.
6 East 39 Street, Suite 900
New York, NY 10016
Att: ORDER DEPT.**